Dating the Damned

Randi-Anne Dey

Dating the Damned

Published in Canada

Randi-Anne Dey Publishing

ISBN

Paperback -978-1-0696816-1-4

eBook - 978-1-0696816-2-1

Two magically doomed weirdos try dating.
They're both terrible at relationships.
The world might end!

Dedication

For the ones who found love in impossible places, and held on even when the world (or Hell) said they shouldn't.

May you stand unbroken, no matter what demons come for you.

Thanks

To everyone who listened when I said,
"So I'm writing about a cursed witch and a demon prince on a dating app…"
And didn't run.
You're the real heroes.
Love you all!

Contents

1. The Witches Curse ... 1

2. Supernatural Soulmates ... 6

3. Brewed for Two ... 12

4. Beastlies ... 20

5. Barter and Blood ... 27

6. Ashen-Guards ... 34

7. Charognis ... 39

8. Hellfire Gardens ... 41

9. Daddy Dearest ... 48

10. Scandel ... 54

11. Charred Bones ... 62

12. The Reluctant Yes ... 71

13. The Wraithmore Estate ... 78

14. Prophetic Curses ... 89

15. Blood Betrayal ... 96

16. Defying the Throne ... 101

17. Destabilizing   106

18. Interference   115

19. Tabloids Altered   122

20. Fire Walks   128

21. Hellbound   140

22. The Reckoning   148

23. Epilogue   156

To everyone who was told not to play with demons.
Do it anyway.
Just make sure you bite harder than they do.

Chapter One

The Witches Curse

Curled up in a blanket on the couch, with the soft crackle of firewood, its warmth filling the air as Zadie turns another page in the book tucked in her lap. She sighs, her mind drifting to the character on the page, just one of many she's fallen for over the years during her quiet, solitary life. A warm flush fills her cheeks as she pictures him standing in the doorway between her kitchen and living room, leaning casually against the frame, dressed in black pants and a white shirt, with sleeves rolled up to his elbows, and the top button undone. With a familiar smirk playing upon his lips, his dark brown eyes catch the firelight and flash gold as they turn her way. Long black hair curled around his shoulders. Tall, dark, and morally grey, just the way she likes them, rather than the sweet, cinnamon roll that doesn't stand a chance with her heart.

"Please tell me you're not mentally undressing another fictional villain."

Zadie jumps, her fingers fumbling to keep the book in her lap. Her cobalt eyes snap toward the source, a smile gracing her lips as she spots her black familiar sprawled across the cushions near the warmth of the fire. "Soot! You scared the crap out of me!"

The cat yawns wide, completely unbothered. "I had to. You've got that glazed-over longing look again. If you drool on that page, I'm not cleaning it."

Leaning over, she places the book down on the table with a sigh, running her fingers through her white-blonde hair and pushing it back off her face. "You know it's the only way I will have a boyfriend, or find love."

"Bah, you are looking in all the wrong places."

"I'm not looking at all, Soot. Not after the last one. Book boyfriends are safe, even if they are fictional."

"So you burned your last one to a crisp. It happens."

"No, it doesn't. When I am out shopping, I see people all the time, living happily with each other. Holding hands, kissing, looking adoringly up at each other. Just like in these books. I am not worth the risk."

"You are worth the risk, Zadie. Do not degrade yourself like that."

"Fine. I will not kill another potential boyfriend because of my curse."

Soot stretches out and flops to his side, lifting his gaze to meet Zadie's. "Zadie, my bonded. I have been with you for how long now?"

"Since I was sixteen."

"Yes, so twelve years. And who have you dated during that time?"

"Josh, Elliot and Desmond..."

"Right. Three..."

"Soot. I can't. I won't have anyone else die because of me."

Soot rises and pads over to the couch. He hops up and crawls into her lap, a soft purr escaping him. "You are allowed to love Zadie. You love me."

"It's not the same. You are my familiar. I am a witch. It's more of a bonding, than true love."

"Ouch, I am hurt."

Zadie reaches over and rubs his head. "You know what I mean."

"I do, and I think you are wrong."

"I'm not. They are all dead because of me. When I fall for them and my emotional connection solidifies, it's like a key or switch clicks inside me. Once that happens, they develop a halo of fate, as I call it, but instead of being good, it's a shimmer of doom around them. One that causes their death exactly seven days after that. As long as I keep my distance, everyone survives. It's best this way."

"You don't know that."

"Yes, I do."

"A car accident killed Josh. Were you driving? No, he was alone in the car. You are not responsible for the truck that t-boned him. Elliot fell off a cliff while out hiking. Reported as a freak accident. Desmond... Yes, well... The whole self-combustion while the two of you kissed in public could have been tied to you, but it might have been something else completely. Another witch who was jealous of what you had? Wrong place at the wrong time? But I will admit, since it was exactly when your lips touched, that is probably the curse."

Zadie closes her eyes and leans back against the couch, letting her head flop against the cushion. Opening her eyes, she stares up at the white ceiling. "It's not an image that leaves easily, Soot. That's why I packed up the apartment five years ago, crossed the country, and bought this cottage in the woods away from everyone and everything. So the world, and especially the tabloids, would forget about me." Her voice wavers as a broken sarcastic edge creeps in, recalling the different tabloids and their harsh words, with her picture plastered all over them. "You saw what they wrote about me... *From Smooch to Scorch, or Passion turns Pyro...*" She let out a short, humorless laugh. "My personal favorite was *Human Goes Boom after Hot Kiss*. Even his last name being Rasgar literally means to tear or ignite. The news was all over that with their headlines too, because some of them actually did their research. *The Rasgar Effect: One Kiss, One Kaboom... Rasgar: Kiss Me, Incinerate Me*. My favorite of his... *Spontaneous Rasgarbustion*."

Soot nuzzles her neck. "Zadie, the answer is right there, in what you just said. You have only dated humans. There are other creatures out there. Supernatural ones... ones not as weak as humans."

"Hey, I am a human."

"You are a human, yes, but also a witch, and your blood has a celestial tinge to it. The distinguishing mark on your back tells you so, along with your looks. Really, it's not your fault some celestial being in your ancestry pissed off another by defying them."

"I am not killing another innocent, Soot. I'm just not."

"Just think about it, alright? When you decide to move away from your fictional boyfriend, which is called fictophilia, by the way, there is a dating app for non-humans. I think it's called Supernatural Soulmates."

"How original."

"Hey, it's better than the others out there. I mean WuvvyDovvy and Thirsttrapz? Gag me up a hairball."

Zadie lifts her head and meets Soots' gaze. "And what happens if there are humans on it? Those dating apps have people all over the world."

"It's not made for humans, Zadie. It's for creatures like us."

"Soot… anyone can write what they want on those and no one's going to know the difference. If it's on the web, humans can apply, and it's not worth the risk."

"It is, but it's not. Look, it's rare that a human stumbles upon our web, and if they do, it's gated to only the shopping aspect. Nothing else. The dating app is beyond that."

"And how do you know all this, Soot?"

Soot shrugs his shoulders and curls up in her lap. "I may or may not play on your laptop while you sleep. There are some gorgeous Ragdolls out there, and the Sphynx. Well, they just strut around hairless. No guessing what's beneath the fur."

"SOOT! I am changing the password!"

"Good luck with that. We are mind-linked, remember?"

"How could I forget? Fine. I will ponder it."

"That's all I can ask. Now, if you are not reading anymore, I am hungry!"

"You are always hungry."

"Yes, but now it's dinnertime, and you have not fed me since breakfast."

Zadie rolls her eyes and picks Soot up, hugging him to her chest as she rises, padding to the kitchen. "And what would his 'Majesty' like for dinner?"

"Whatever you are having?"

"Peanut butter and banana sandwiches."

"That is not dinner! Now make us something decent."

She laughs and sets him on the counter. Opening the cupboard over her head, she rummages around in it and pulls out a package of cat treats and places it in front of him. "I bought you something the last time I was at the store. Dried sardines."

Soots' eyes widen as he bats the bag with his paw. "Really? I haven't had these in forever."

"I know. I haven't seen them. It seems another company is putting them out now. You can have one after dinner."

"Zee! You are evil! Open it now!"

Laughing, she pats the top of his head. "Fine, my spoiled one. If only to keep you quiet while I am making dinner."

"Deal!"

She picks up the bag, tears it open, and pulls out five sardines, placing them on the counter in front of him. After sealing the bag, she tucks it back into the cupboard and sets about making dinner, smiling at the soft purrs and growls of contentment Soot makes as he devours his treat. Later, after dinner, she settles into the living room once more, book in hand, trying to focus on the written words in front of her, but her mind drifts elsewhere, replaying Soot's comments about dating a supernatural.

Chapter Two

Supernatural Soulmates

Two days later, Zadie sits at her laptop and looks over the magical orders on her website. She sighs inwardly, knowing she's going to be busy this afternoon fulfilling them, and then tomorrow with shipping them off. Her eyes stray to Soot lounging on the windowsill, basking in the sunbeam, his tail twitching in delight, recalling his words from earlier this week.

Opening another tab, she searches through to the dating site, her eyes widening at some of the advertised profile pictures there. She picks up a piece of paper and fans herself as she shifts back to her website tab. What is she doing? She is cursed. She can't risk dating. Some of them look as if they stepped out of her fantasy books and into the real world. Not that supernaturals don't live here, they do, just not ones like that! They work hard to blend in with humans; not to look like a fae warrior, here to rescue a damsel in distress, sword and all. Flipping back, she stares at the pictures, chewing on her lip as she looks up to the create account button.

"Do it!"

"Soot! Are you eavesdropping on my thoughts again?"

"Zee. Any magical being within three miles will hear those thoughts! It's interrupting my sunbathing!"

"Fine!" She mutters beneath her breath as she shifts the mouse across the screen, hesitating at the create account button, before finally clicking it. An hour later, she stares at her profile, or rather, the submit button, wondering if she dares. Supernatural Soulmates claims to pair magically inclined beings with an 86% success rate, some even with dangerous levels of compatibility. That means her odds are more than good at finding someone, but then the odds are also good that she might kill them.

"If you don't click the submit button, I will. Stop hesitating and get on with it."

"What if it doesn't work, Soot?"

"What if it does? Besides, at least with a supernatural being, you can be honest and tell them about the curse. If they run, they are not worth it."

"Soot, I would run if I knew death was an outcome of dating them."

"That's because you haven't found the right person yet, Zadie. When you do, you will know it and together, you will take the world by storm."

"Or destroy it." She mutters softly. "You know I have already seen upcoming disasters occurring in the world, and it's usually when I am on a date with someone. Since I stopped dating, the visions stopped. Now that you have put this in my brain and I am considering it, flickers have returned. Soot, I can't even think of being romantically involved out there in the world. If I do, bad things happen. Milk sours, birds drop dead out of the surrounding sky, cars crash. I am only safe here, alone with you."

"All coincidences. Milk goes bad all the time. I know. You've tried to feed me some. Living creatures die. So some died while you were in the area. You have no proof it was actually you."

"I do. I saw a cute guy walking down the street and wondered what a date would be like. Then six birds fell from the sky. I tucked my head and scurried off the other way."

"I recall you telling me about it. But didn't you also say one farmer was spraying something in the field? It could have been toxic to them and just bad timing."

"Or it was me."

Soot rises and arches his back, turning his other side to face the sun. "It's possible. The only way to find out is to hit submit."

Her fingers twitch on the mouse; her inner sass dares her to hit the button while sanity yells at her to stop and delete the application. Closing her eyes, she takes a deep breath and opts to listen to her darker side, having had enough of being alone. She watches the words flash upon her screen as she clicks the submit button. *Thank you for joining Supernatural Soulmates, where sparks fly, curses break, and love might just literally set your soul on fire. Whether you're a vampire looking for a heartbeat, a witch tired of warlocks, or a demon seeking something hotter than Hell, we've got your match. Swipe right at your own risk.*

"Well done, Zadie. Now it's just a matter of time before matches show up."

"You don't know that." The pit of her stomach clenches as nausea rises in her throat. Rising, she bolts outside, heading for her sacred herb garden, dry heaving at the stress flooding her body. Sinking down to her knees in the center, she forces herself to breathe deeply, feeling her magical space calm her as she mutters to herself. "It's alright, Zadie. No one will apply when death is on the table. Compared to them, I am just a dull human. In a week, I can close the app and return to my book boyfriends, and pretend this never happened."

An hour later, she returns to the cottage, herbs in hand and feeling better. She heads to the kitchen and places them on the counter, knowing the only way to stop feeling sorry for herself is to focus on her orders for the duration of the day. Potions first, then enchanted stones and whatever else is remaining is left to tomorrow.

***

The next morning, Zadie wakes her laptop up, seeing a new message in her inbox from Supernatural Soulmates. Clicking it open, she reads her email, stating a match has been made and to log in to her account to view it. Sighing, she tabs over to the app, reading the warning flashing across her screen.

Compatibility: 89%. Potentially apocalyptic with a high risk of cosmic fallout.

She laughs softly at the accuracy of the words, daring to swipe right to view her match's profile. A gasp escapes her as she stares into copper eyes, peering out from behind a black hoodie covering most of his face. His smile, if you can call it that, is clearly arrogant, with the tips of fangs showing at the corners. A vampire? Interesting that they would pair her up with one that feeds on blood.

"Demon."

Zadie snaps her gaze around, spotting Soot lying on the back of the couch, peering over her shoulder. "How do you know?"

"Cause it says so in the description, which you have not read because you are staring at the picture. Besides, he has color in his skin. A vampire doesn't. They are usually pasty white. That and a vampire's eyes are dark and steal your soul. I feel no such vibe coming from those copper orbs. In fact, I sense he could be a good match for you."

Zadie rolls her eyes. "Yes, an 89% match, and you can't tell that by a profile."

"I can. He's special. You're special. It's perfect."

"Why do you think he's special?"

"Copper is a rarity in the demonic world. Usually, their eyes are red. His posture shows breeding, even if it's hidden within a hoodie."

"How do you know all this, Soot?"

"I am a familiar. Magic school does train us before they send us out to find our witch or warlock."

Zadie sighs softly. "Sorry, I didn't mean to question you, Soot."

Soot jumps off the couch and pads over to the chair, hopping up into her lap. He rubs his face into her neck. "It's quite alright. I feel your stress, but I believe it's misplaced. Just go on one date. No emotional commitment."

"Fine, you win." She leans forward and types a message, telling her match that she will meet him at the *Bean There, Hexed That Café,* tomorrow afternoon at three. This way, if things go haywire, there are witches manning the place to put out any potential disasters. Sending it off, she looks down at Soot in her lap. "Are you happy now?"

"Meh, I think you should have set the date for later today."

"He might be busy, and who knows how often he checks his profile? Tomorrow is better all around."

"I bet he checks it a few times a day." Soot jumps off her lap and winds his way through her legs.

"Great, now that you have done that, let's have breakfast. Then we can work on your orders."

"I think you would eat 24-7 if I allowed it, Soot." Zadie laughs and rises from her chair, heading to the kitchen to start her day.

Soot pads along behind her. "That I would."

She spends the day in silence, puttering around her house, cleaning, sorting, creating. Trying to force her thoughts off the date, she has just set up for the next day and the growing anxiety building as the hours pass.

***

Zadie pulls out of sleep with a pit of dread coiling in her stomach at the thought of her date later that day. Groaning, she rolls over, swiping at the heat prickling her skin and the fine sheen of sweat clinging to it. A low, rumbling purr draws her gaze to Soot, lounging on the pillow in the corner of her bed. "This is such a bad idea," she mutters. "I should cancel."

"No, you shouldn't. For your own sake, you need to go through with this."

"Soot, I haven't been on a date in five years!"

"And that's exactly why you need to do this. Look, I understand it's stressful. I feel it running rampant throughout our bond, and I am willing to bet he is feeling the same thing as you. You are both strangers, meeting each other for the first time. Go drink some chamomile tea and calm those nerves. Then make us some breakfast. After that, we can go through your closet and decide what would be best for a first date in a coffee shop."

"Soot! I was just going to wear jeans and a shirt."

"Zadie, my witch, my devotion, my bonded. That is exactly why you are still single."

"No, I am still single because I am cursed."

"Zadie, enough. If it doesn't work out, I won't push you anymore. How about that?"

Drawing in a deep breath, she holds it for a few moments before exhaling. "Deal." Rising from the bed, she sets about making herself busy, trying to ignore the fact that she has a date with a potential demon later in the day.

Just before three, Zadie steps into the café, dressed in black tights with an oversized dark blue sweater. Silver bells dangle from a chain wrapped around her knee-high black boots, matching the ones around her neck and wrist. Soot's choice, along with the winged eyeliner and lip gloss, both of which she desired to rub off her face. The whole doomed package, he said, and she had foolishly gone along with him. To what? Date a demon? More like a garden-variety half-elf illusionist with mommy issues or a spell-slinging vampire cosplayer. Either way, even if he has a hint of human blood, she is out of here.

Drawn from her thoughts by the rich scent of burnt cinnamon and lavender, Zadie takes a slow breath. The gentle murmur of conversation hums around her, not loud enough to overwhelm, but just enough to be comforting if her date goes sideways. Her eyes skim over the crowd, looking for someone who matches the profile photo from the app. A sigh of relief escapes her at not seeing them. If Lady-Luck is with her, she can get her London Fog, wait the polite fifteen minutes and return home.

Her gaze lingers on the bookshelves along the back wall and the cozy couches nestled beside them. Filled of course with the usual book club regulars, one she considered joining briefly. The idea was tempting until she buried it under the same logic she always used: a solitary life is safer. Easier. Less combustible. And yet... here she is, about to go on her first date in five years.

She offers a smile to the barista and places her order, then moves to the collection counter. Drink in hand, she chooses an empty table and sinks into a chair. Cold iron, masked beneath a layer of lead and mint green paint, makes her skin prickle. A clever disguise for the grounding metal, designed to contain dark magic. Iron horseshoes hang discreetly above each door and window, while narrow trails of salt trace the baseboard, magically sealed to ensure they stay unbroken. It's why this place is so popular with the magical community. And why she chose it. The protective wards might help keep her curse in check. Not that it should show up on a first date.

She stirs her drink and blends the whipped cream into it, watching it bubble ominously, knowing her nerves are the cause. Relax, she tells herself mentally. You'll make awkward conversation, fake a phone call, and go home to microwave leftover pasta in peace.

Chapter Three

Brewed for Two

Then the door opens, drawing everyone's attention as the temperature inside rises five degrees. In walks a very tall man in a black hoodie that reads *Hell's Kitchen - Family Owned Since 666*, dark jeans, and boots heavy enough to double as small weapons. Two neat black horns curl back from his temples, standing out against his chestnut hair that reaches his shoulders. He looks... confused, and oddly hopeful, like a freshly summoned demon trying not to scare the summoner. His copper eyes scan the café, landing on her, sitting alone at the table, a smile spreading across his face.

Zadie blinks, knowing instantly that he's trouble as she feels her heart rate increase and a cold sweat forms on her palms. Clutching the cup, she watches him ignore the other patrons and weave his way over to her. All instincts within scream at her to run. To bolt back to her car, and high-tail it out of here, never to look back. But her gaze lifts to his as he stands before her, drawn to their copper depths, feeling the connection before words are even spoken.

"Snow Lily?"

"You must be Hellion Royale," she says, not missing how even the café lights seem to shudder at the weight of his voice.

"Yes, but I go by Zevran to my friends. I brought you something." He pulls a small bouquet from behind his back, a handful of blackened stems and something possibly still hissing, wrapped in black paper.

"Zadie..." Her gaze shifts to the plants. "Is that screaming nightshade?"

He glances down at it sheepishly. "Yes, it's traditional in Hell. What one would call a romantic gesture. Do you not like it?"

"Of course I do. It's just a surprise, that's all. These are scarce. They only exist in the royal gardens, from what I hear."

"I know. I picked them just for you." He extends his arm, offering the bouquet.

Feeling her heart skip a beat, she smiles and takes the bouquet from him, careful not to let her fingers stray too close to the very-much-alive flowers which she knows will happily bite one or two off, and that's without counting the thorned stems that drink like vampires. She sets the bouquet on the table beside her, then gestures to the chair before reclaiming her mug. "Have a seat."

"Thank you." His eyes drop to Zadie's hands, practically strangling the mug in her hands. "I should get myself a drink first."

"Right, sorry. I arrived earlier than expected. I should have waited."

"No, I get it. I would have done the same. Personal protection, in case the date doesn't show up."

Zadie smiles, feeling a weakening in her defenses. "Yes, it doesn't look as bad sitting here waiting with a drink versus empty-handed."

"Be right back." He heads to the counter and places his order, returning a few minutes later with an espresso in hand. He pulls the chair out and plops down, his eyes studying Zadie for a moment. "I've never done this before. The dating thing, that is. I mean, it's not like I haven't been on dates, just not app ones like this. More like hookups between demons."

Zadie subtly covers her drink, hearing its soft growls amidst the bubbling milk, mentally reciting a protection aura and wielding its magic around her cup. "That's fine. I've only ever had boyfriends burst into flames."

"Ah. A metaphor?"

"Err... No."

He pauses, his eyes darkening as he grows thoughtful. "So you are dangerous, like your profile stated."

"If you can call it that. I'm cursed."

"So am I."

"Somehow I doubt that."

"I am. I have a chaotic energy around me that warps reality. It does things, breaks things, makes drinks growl..." As if on cue, somewhere in the café, a mirror cracks. "What I am trying to say is that everyone has their quirks. When I get really nervous, I accidentally summon Hell-beasts. Dad wants me to settle down with someone in hopes it might lessen the chaos around me."

"I think Hell-beasts would be better. Every guy I've kissed dies."

"Technically, I'm already damned, so... loophole?"

Zadie chuckles quietly at his words, even if they are true. "Do you want to take that risk?"

"I showed up, didn't I? Your profile was most intriguing."

Her gaze shifts to the barista pulling the mirror off the wall, seeing the vision of doom reflecting upon its surface, then over to the statue beside the counter, its eyes weeping, with tears rolling down its cheeks. Averting her eyes, she shakily lifts the cup to her lips, taking a drink as she processes her thoughts, opting for the safest option. Placing the cup down, she leans across the table towards him, knowing what she had written in her profile. Enough so that the average person would swipe left and pass, and yet, this man... demon... made the choice to risk it. "Look, Zevran. I don't think this is going to work. I joined the app out of spite and seasonal depression. That and my familiar, Soot, pushed me into it. You seem... stable, which means you should probably run."

Zevran sips his espresso as if it is the most natural thing in the world. He tilts his head and studies her. "Supernatural Soulmates stated this match has an 89% chance of cataclysm."

Zadie rolls her eyes and glances down at her cup. "Great. Maybe we'll destroy the universe by going Dutch over drinks."

Zevran chuckles. "You make the apocalypse sound charming. Perhaps we should save it for dinner."

A long pause stretches between them. The lights dim again; this time not for ambiance. Outside, the drizzle has twisted into a localized thundercloud, blood-red and circling solely above the café.

Zadie exhales, her eyes flicking to the storm. She knows what he's doing by offering a second date. Did she want that? Her gaze drifts back to him, torn between the magnetic pull of curiosity and the familiar urge to bolt back to her quiet cottage.

"Dinner, huh?" She arches an eyebrow. "Wanna see what happens if we hold hands first before you commit to that?"

Zevran looks at her as if she's handed him the moon. "Very much."

Their fingers touch and the earth trembles, causing the people in the café to panic; some pulling out their phones to call friends, while others hide under the tables, expecting the roof to collapse on them.

"Wait... if I kiss you, will it break the curse or trigger the end of the world?" Zevran looks in awe at the woman before him, feeling the mate sparks bonding them at their touch.

Panic tightens Zadie's chest as she yanks her hand back, staring at Zevran in shock. Did he not see what even their touch did, and now he wants to kiss her? She rubs her hand, trying to numb the tingling feeling from where their skin connected. A sensation created when soulmates meet and often reserved only for shifters. Not humans like her, and certainly not with a demon.

"I'm sorry, I can't do this." She rises from the chair and tries to run from the café, only to feel a powerful grasp wrapping around her waist and pulling her into a hard chest. Smoke and brimstone surround her, settling the frantic pace of her heart. She closes her eyes as her body shudders against his warmth, resting up against him. Her whisper slips out, filled with pain and agony at already falling for her date. "Please let me go."

"Zadie, my sweet mate. Don't run from me. Now that I have found you, I am never letting you go."

She leans her head back, tilting her cheek to rest against his chest. "You might die?"

"It's a risk I am willing to take."

"The world might end."

"Then we live in mine. Daddy won't let a simple curse destroy the underworld. Our being together might even cause more fire and brimstone, which he will love. I will admit, he wanted me to settle down with some lesser demon, and while I don't know what he will think of a human, he will see the mate bond for what it is. The chaos we cause will only add to his love of you. It's destiny, don't you see?"

"Yes, a destiny to destroy each other. Practically a romantic Hell-storm."

"That's the nicest thing anyone's ever said to me." He turns her around, his hand lingering on her waist as he meets her gaze while the other caresses her cheek gently, his eyes darkening in desire.

Zadie closes her eyes, feeling the flames settle into her body, before panic takes over once more. Seeing him leaning in for a kiss, she ducks out of his arms and bolts from the cafe. The storm outside pounds down upon her, as if it is trying to drive her back into the cafe. She leans into the winds, feeling the rain soak through her as she makes her way to her car, where she fumbles to get the keys in the lock. "Please, car, open."

Hearing the locks click, she slips in and closes the door, brushing her wet hair out of her face as she glances toward the cafe, seeing Zevran standing there in confusion. Sliding the keys in the ignition, she backs up and pulls out onto the road; not daring to look back because if she does, she'll return to his side, and it isn't safe.

Once outside the radius of the storm, she floors it, making it home in record time. Stepping into the safety of her home, her eyes catch Soot's shocked expression. "Don't ask."

"Did it not go well?"

"It did."

"Then why are you here and not with him?"

"Soot. I don't want to discuss it." She hangs her keys on the hook by the door, and stumbles into her room, stripping out of her wet clothes. Heading to the bathroom, she grabs a towel to dry off before pulling on her comfy casuals.

Soot jumps onto the bed and watches her. "Zadie, what happened?"

Zadie pads back and sits on the bed, pulling a pillow into her arms and hugging it tightly. She rests her chin on it as she tilts her gaze over to her familiar. "He's my mate."

"He's what?"

"You know, the other half of my soul, sort of thing. The sparks that fly when you touch each other. The kind humans like me don't get!"

Soot wanders over and rubs against her. "Again, I ask, why are you here and not with him?"

"I don't want him to die, Soot. How many people have to die because I am cursed? Three is enough. I don't want to make him number four."

"You won't."

"How can you be sure?"

"Because he's your soulmate. Fate would not be that cruel."

"It has so far. Look at me, everyone I get attached to dies. How is that not cruel?"

"It's a curse. Not fate. Bad ancestry, if you will."

"I don't know, Soot."

"Look, he's a demon. Technically, he's not in the land of the living like humans are."

Zadie offers Soot a wry smile. "Yes, he said that too. Called it a loophole, but I won't take the risk."

"What's the worst that will happen? He returns to Hell and just comes back."

"No, then he's stuck there for like 101 years."

"Not if he dies... only if you banish him, and I don't see you doing that to your mate."

"Is it not the same thing?"

"Not even close. Dying returns his soul back to the underworld, where he hails from. Then, he just reforms and portal steps back. Banishment is casting him back and locking him down in Hell."

"See, there's that loophole. I don't know what my magic will do to him. It might banish him. All three previous deaths were different. Car crash, fall, combustion. We don't know whether banishment is an option."

"There is that. I will look into it."

"See, I told you. It's safer this way."

"I think you are making a mistake."

"Soot, please..." She lifts her head to the knock on the door. Furrowing her brows, she places the pillow aside and pads out to the main room. Peeking out the window, her heart flutters at the sight of Zevran standing there, her bouquet in his hands.

She lets the curtain flutter back, wringing her hands about whether to open the door, when she hears his voice.

"Zadie, I know you are in there. Right behind the door, in fact. Please open up."

Zadie reaches for the door and opens it, her eyes darkening as they roam over Zevran, before locking them on the bouquet in his hands. "How did you find me?"

Zevran grins, holding the bouquet out to her. "You left these behind."

She accepts the flowers, fiddling with the wrapping. "You didn't answer my question."

"You are my mate. Now that we have met, you are like a beacon, calling to me. I can't ignore it."

"Please, I can't."

"No." He places his fingers on her lips, tilting his head at the sound of a tree crashing in the forest nearby, and pulls his touch away. "Why did you run, Zadie?"

Her eyes skip to the woods, feeling the wind picking up in the surrounding air. "I don't want to kill you."

"Honestly, you can't kill me, Zadie. But if it makes you feel better. How about we go downstairs tomorrow and talk to my father? If his answers don't satisfy you, we can visit an oracle."

Zadie lifts her gaze up to his copper eyes, reading the sincerity and concern within them. She draws in a deep breath, feeling their bond traveling through her, as her skin prickles, finding herself giving a nod of agreement. "Alright. We can talk to him."

Zevran shifts backwards as a potted plant rolls between them and winks her way. "It's windy here."

"It's because you touched me."

He winks. "I know. I can't wait to see this out."

Zadie smiles, shaking her head. "You like chaos."

"Of course!"

"Are you sure it's a bond to me, and not a bond to chaos?"

Zevran lifts a hand to his chin, tapping it lightly as he pretends to consider her question. His copper eyes twinkle mischievously as he smirks Zadie's way. "Now, that's a tough choice. I might need to take a night to ponder it."

Zadie bursts out laughing. "You are so bad."

"Well, I do hail from down-under. It's in my soul!" Zevran bows, winking her way. "Now that I have brought a laugh to your lips and a smile back to your eyes, I must part ways. I will pick you up tomorrow? Mid-afternoon?"

Zadie nods, "I will be here. That gives me time to complete some of my orders in the morning."

Zevran reaches for her hand, only to pull back as thunder rolls across the sky. "Right. Enjoy your day, my darling mate." He smiles and shimmers, his copper eyes the last to fade away as he returns to his realm.

Chapter Four

Beastlies

Z adie stares outside, her eyes watching the storm roll out just as quickly as it rolled in. Closing the door, she turns to find Soot perched on the back of the couch watching her. "What!"

"I can feel the chemistry between the two of you."

"You cannot!" She pivots and stomps into the kitchen, looking for a vase to put the nightshade in.

"You know those need dirt, right?"

"I know that!" Zadie stops, narrowing her eyes at her familiar, and marches through the kitchen to the back patio.

"That's not what your thoughts were saying. You were going for water, and I would rather not listen to their complaints for the duration of their lives."

"They are not dying on me."

"Really, because you seem to think everything dies around you, and I'm still here."

Zadie slides to a stop, twisting her body to glare at her familiar. "That's not fair, and you know it."

"It's perfectly fair, and you need to start accepting it. When you get those beasts in dirt, bring them back in and put them on the kitchen windowsill. They need morning light."

"Soot! I would rather not discuss this."

"That's because you know I am right. When you are ready to consider it, you can find me in the bedroom picking out tomorrow's outfit for you."

"Wait, what?"

"Clearly, your mate is royalty. Only they can pick the screaming nightshade."

"He mentioned his daddy ruled down there."

"Ah. You snared yourself a princeling. The question is, which one?"

"How many are there?"

"Six."

"Of course there are." Zadie rolls her eyes and steps out onto the back porch, bare feet brushing against the weathered boards. Her gaze sweeps over the mismatched planters lining the rail, each one home to something magical, before she debates which unlucky pot will house the little beasts.

She wanders between the rows, brushing against curling leaves and swiping away the faint shimmer of pollen that hangs in the warm evening air. Spotting an empty planter, she scoops it up and carries it over to her worktable; a sun-bleached, paint-chipped relic that has seen better decades. The wood is warped and pitted from rain and sun, but it's still solid, a loyal old servant to her peculiar gardening habits.

Placing the bouquet down, she sets the pot beside it and grabs a bag of dirt from beneath it. She sinks her fingers into the soil, tilling it in slow, practiced motions. The smell of damp earth rises around her, grounding and rich. The nightshades in their temporary container give a low, leafy hiss, their tiny thorned vines twitching like impatient snakes.

"Look," she mutters, tilting her head at them as though reason might persuade them, "you want proper plantation, you're going to have to wait. And don't even think about taking my fingers off while I transfer you, or I *will* dunk you in water. Is that clear?"

A rustle of leaves answers her, followed by two softer hisses, almost… agreeable.

"That's what I thought."

Once the dirt is ready, she unwraps the bouquet, inspecting each flower. The cut edges are already sprouting delicate rootlets, pale tendrils reaching toward the soil as if they can smell it. Carefully, she nests them in the dirt, leaving just enough space between each plant to keep the peace.

She folds the bouquet paper into a neat square, tucking it into her pocket, and lifts the pot. Halfway to the house, a tickle brushes the side of her neck. She jerks the pot away and stares down at the flowers, whose petals sway toward her, the tips brushing her skin again in a feather-light caress.

Inside, she sets the pot on the windowsill. This time when she reaches out, the flowers lean into her touch, petals pressing against her fingers in something suspiciously like a nuzzle.

"Okay," she says slowly, a reluctant smile tugging at her lips as she caresses along the velvet petals, "you might be kinda adorable. I will make some sweet milk for your soil tomorrow." Pulling the square of paper out, she hesitates dropping it into the recycle bin. Her fingers trace over the embossed flowers as she carries it back to the living room. Settling on the couch with a sigh, she pulls the paper up to her nose, and sniffs it, catching the faint scent of brimstone along its edges.

Placing it down on the table, she shifts her eyes to the bedroom door, watching her clothes floating around the room. "Soot! What are you doing?"

"I told you, deciding on your outfit for tomorrow."

"Nothing too fancy, or too hot."

"Fancy yes, hot no, and I think I have just the right one." Soot jumps off the bed, followed by an ankle length, flowing gown with long bell-sleeves, inset with lace panels. Black as obsidian but threaded with subtle crimson and ember-gold embroidery in arcane patterns, it catches the light like smoldering coals. Behind it, a single pendant, glowing faintly with protective magic. Alongside that, a belt made of interlinked sigil-shaped metal pieces, matching the black leather zip boots, with a chunky heel, almost like a witch's armor.

"Soot! I am not wearing that! That's evening attire!"

"Yes, you are. You haven't worn this in ages."

"There is a reason for that. I am just going to wear tights and an oversized shirt. Like today."

"No, you are not. This is not a first date. It's setting boundaries when you meet Daddy. This outfit tells him you are confident in who you are, and kick ass enough not to put up with any bullshit, even if he is the king of Hell."

Zadie rolls her eyes as the dress lands in her lap, running her fingers over the silky fabric, recalling when she bought it on a whim at the witches convention. She had tried it on in the stall, and loved it, despite the price tag on it. She put it on one other time, intending to wear it out to dinner on a date, but her date cancelled at the last minute, which in hindsight, probably saved his life. Instead, she wore it around the house for an hour and packed it at the back of her closet. And that's where it ended up when she moved everything here, hidden away and forgotten about. "I don't know, Soot. Don't you think this is a bit too much?"

"Not at all. This dress will earn you the respect you deserve, and Zevran will love it."

"How do you know his name?"

"Bonded, remember...besides, it's coming through loud and clear, along with thoughts I don't want to hear. I get enough when you read your romance novels."

"Sorry, it's just, how can I be this attracted to him already?"

"Mate bond."

"I get that. I have read enough about them; I just never thought it was so real."

"Oh, it's very real, and no matter how much you try to resist, it will call to you. You won't be able to ignore it."

"Great."

Soot jumps onto the couch beside her. "Zadie, this is a good thing."

"Is it though?"

"It is."

"I guess we'll see."

***

The next morning, Zadie wakes up with a muffled groan, pulling the comforter over her head and burying her face in the pillow. Is she ready to meet the King of Hell or perhaps the better question is... Is she ready to see Zevran again? No to the first but yes to the second, even if it creates a storm of chaotic energy around them, ranging from the storm outside the coffee shop to the winds here that toppled some of her trees and potted plants.

Rolling out of bed with a groan, she makes her way to the kitchen for her morning tea, pausing at the nightshades, which are hissing softly in the window. "Good morning, my little flowering beasts." She chuckles as they rustle and twist toward her, turning away from the sunlight in the window while she sets her tea to brew. "Right, I believe I promised you some sweet milk today."

Padding to the fridge, she pulls out a container of goat's milk and places it on the counter with a soft thud. Rifling through her cupboards, she collects a jar of honey, a tin of cinnamon, and a small clay pot of wood ash. From the hanging rack above her kitchen island, she lifts a small dented pot, its bottom blackened from years of use, and sets it gently on the stove.

Turning the burner on, she measures a cup of milk and pours it into the pot, along with one teaspoon of cinnamon and one of ash. She leans in and sniffs, enjoying the smoky spice floating from the pot as it dissolves into the warming milk. As it bubbles, she spoons out a quarter cup of thick honey, folding it into the milk with a lazy swirl and stirring constantly.

Once the mixture turns a uniform, golden beige, she removes it from the heat and pours it into a shallow ceramic bowl and sets it by the open window to catch a cooling breeze. Her eyes shift over to the nightshades, who are practically quivering with anticipation. "Patience, it's too hot for you." She pauses, suddenly realizing they are from Hell and questioning her words about whether it is too hot. "Then again, it might not be, but since you can't actually speak, you need to wait till it's cooler. I am not burning your little roots because I actually like you."

She reaches out to pet a few of them, earning a grumbling hiss from the others. "I cannot believe I have jealous flowers!" Ensuring she pets them all at least once, she moves over to her coffee pot, one that has never percolated coffee in its life, and pours herself a cup of vanilla tea. Turning, she smiles at the plants, each bending its stalk to the milk sitting nearby, trying to reach their treat. "I am going to water the plants out back. You can have it after."

As she steps out of the kitchen, she can hear the discontented hisses from the plants, bringing a smile to her lips. If nothing else works with Zevran, at least she received an amazing gift. Twenty minutes later, she returns from watering and sets her empty teacup on the ivory counter. She lifts the bowl and pours the milk into the dirt, smiling at their antics as their stalks sway and their leaves flutter, as if dancing in delight. "There, that should keep you happy for a few days. Now, I have orders I need to get done before my trip to your world this afternoon. Try to be good."

Crossing the kitchen to the pantry door on the other side, she opens it and steps inside the small room she had shifted to her apothecary. Taking a moment, she breathes in deep, savoring the scent of warm beeswax, the sharp tang of rosemary, the faint metallic prickle of magic that lingers, along with the blend of herbs, hanging on strings, drying in the air.

Moving towards the bookshelf, which houses a mixture of books, small clay pots, and glass jars, she pulls a few down and turns towards her work table, which is half-buried beneath yesterday's clutter. An open mortar with dried yarrow petals still clinging to the sides, a bundle of wolfsbane in wax paper and four bunches of lavender from her garden out back.

Zadie exhales, the tension in her shoulders easing just a fraction. Here, in her magical space, with a single stained glass window she had installed, she didn't have to answer to anyone. Not even her thoughts about whether she should risk accepting Zevran as a mate. Or that his father is the King of Hell and she's meeting him today. Only her magical concoctions and the order list beside her, waiting to be filled.

She spends the morning working her way through people's requests. Once they are complete, she labels and packages them, before setting them aside to be popped into the mail. Nearing lunchtime, she finishes her last one and packs everything up.

Stepping back into the kitchen, her gaze shifts to the nightshade, swaying gently back and forth in the sunlight. She chuckles inwardly, thinking if plants could be drunk, then this was a prime example of that. Making herself a sandwich, she sits at the small wooden table and eats her lunch, feeling the happiness radiating off her plants.

"Right, I guess I should stop watching you sway and get my ass in gear and get ready for the one that gave you to me. See you later, little beasties!" Dropping her dishes in the sink, she pads out of the kitchen towards the bathroom. Having had a quick shower, she dries herself off and steps into the bedroom, her eyes drifting to Soot, curled up in her pillows. "Lazy morning?"

"I'm a cat. I am always lazy."

"That's true." She answers as she sets about dressing in what Soot had paraded for her last night. Finishing her hair and makeup, she moves to inspect herself in the mirror.

Zadie adjusts the gown and stares at herself in the mirror; her white hair loose and falling down in waves around her shoulders. Smokey makeup around her eyes with a pale tan lipstick. The dress hugs her curves and flows out past her hips to just above her ankles. The gold and crimson thread flickers like fire as she moves, matching the fire pendant at her throat. Each is an ode to the fire of Hell she is walking into. Chunky boots match her belt, finishing the look for her witchy vibes.

At the knock on her door, Zadie turns her gaze from the mirror, glancing at Soot. "Are you sure this is not too much?"

"It's perfect. It has class, but not to the point of being overdressed. One that says, you know who you are and how to handle any situation. Besides, even if it's not all those things, it's 100% you." Soot gives a nod and points to the door. "Now go."

Chapter Five

Barter and Blood

A sudden prickle of unease runs along her skin, raising the fine hairs on her arms. She rubs them absently as she pads toward the front door. The hinges give a soft groan as she pulls it open, and there he is. Boots planted wide, black leather pants molded to him like a second skin, and a deep wine dress shirt with the top three buttons left carelessly undone. The rich fabric encourages her to run her fingers along it and play with the open buttons. A far cry from the hoodie and jeans he wore on the first date.

Her gaze lifts slowly to meet the pull of his molten-copper eyes. That one wayward lock of hair falls across his brow, infuriatingly perfect. Her hands twitch at her side as she fights the ridiculous urge to push it aside.

"Zevran..."

"Wow Zadie. You look... Well amazing. That dress is perfect for you."

A blush crosses her cheeks as she fidgets beneath his gaze, tucking part of her body against the doorjamb. "Thank you."

Zevran smirks, pushing the lock out of his eyes only to have it fall back into place. "Not used to compliments, I see."

Zadie stiffens her spine, lifting her eyes to meet his. "Why do you say that?"

"The adorable blush across your cheeks and your body posture indicate you want to hide. You are beautiful, Zadie, and I am not just saying that because you are my mate. When I walked into that coffee shop, even tucked in the corner, you drew my attention. Remember, I live with succubuses, who many say are the most beautiful creatures that walk the realms, and yet, they do not compare to you."

Zadie lifts her hand, holding it palm out. "Okay. You don't need to lay it on so thick."

Zevran smiles. "It's not thick if it's the truth. Accept it for what it is."

Zadie sighs, slumping against the doorframe. "Sorry. You are right. It's just that the last three men I got attached to are dead, and only one of them felt I deserved compliments. Since the last one exploded when I kissed him, I packed up, moved here, and now I pretty much hide in my cabin."

"Lucky number three."

"It's not lucky, and I don't want you to be number four."

Zevran chuckles and reaches out to take her hand. "I would be number four, five, and six if it meant that you trusted me. I am here for the long haul, Zadie."

Zadie chews her lip, her gaze dropping to his hand, fighting the internal war and losing. She slips her fingers into his and steps outside, only for the door to slam against her backside, pushing her closer to him. From the kitchen window, the nightshades screech, their shrill cries brimming with jealousy at the contact.

The next second, heat engulfs her along with the din of chatter. "Where are we?"

"Hell's market. I thought we could spend some time together before hitting the castle."

Chaos energy flows out from them as a nearby awning collapses. Zadie jumps as the floating jars next to her suddenly drop, shattering with bright bursts of sulfur flame.

Zevran yanks her away from the shattering glass, only to hear the groan of ironwood shifting, followed by the sharp crack as it snaps. A beast of burden pulling a cart suddenly belches fire, setting a nearby stall's canopy ablaze until someone beats it out with wings. A merchant with chains is showing off wares when one suddenly writhes to life and coils around his leg, dragging him halfway down the street before he beats it back into submission.

Zadie pulls out of Zevran's grasp, standing in the middle of the chaos, while ash-rain drifts from above, settling in her hair and upon her skin, only to vanish in a hiss of steam seconds later. "Ok enough. No touching here either."

Zevran grins. "Not enjoying the chaos?"

"No."

"This is pretty common around here. It's not like they will care."

"It doesn't matter. I know it's us."

"Alright Zadie. We will do it your way. No touching. Shall we walk?"

Zadie walks along beside Zevran, resisting the urge to reach out and take his hand, or walk with his arm draped over her shoulder like normal couples do. She can feel the ground pulses like a heartbeat, sending ripples through the cobblestones, enough to throw her balance off for a step or two.

She catches the looks shifting in her direction, uncertain whether it is because she's a human, walking around in Hell, or if it's who she's walking with. A bit of both, she supposes, especially with the desire-filled looks cast his way, or the way their eyes roam over his body.

She stops at a few booths, intrigued by the merchandise here, some of which she never expected. Picking up a stuffed creature with horns, she turns it over in her hands and looks over at Zevran. "Stuffies? In Hell?"

Zevran chuckles. "Just because we are demons, doesn't mean we are not unlike you humans. Half the souls here are reincarnations of human souls. They crave comforts from home, and the merchants here provide it."

She places the plushie down and looks around, the black stone beneath her feet, the small sparks floating through the air, like fireflies fluttering around. Cressets on tall metal poles burn, casting an orange glow all around them. Yurts and pavilions stretch as far as she can see, each with a table out front, and a demon hawking wares. Her gaze lingers on the stall across from them, noticing a vendor selling bottled wedding vows in jars, each whispering a different promise. "That's... creepy."

"Some have no imagination and need help in that department. It's our version of the internet. So what do you think?"

"It's not what I expected."

"Let me guess. You expected fields of lava spewing fire and brimstone, air plagued with sulphuric smoke, and tormented souls, locked in hanging cages, wailing in dismay. Perhaps red dragons spewing forth more flames while we dance in the fires and laugh maniacally." As he talks, a Hellhound breaks loose from its handler, scattering shoppers before Zevran growls and the beast instantly stops.

The handler gives a nod of appreciation and leashes the dog, dragging it back to its stall.

"Partly, yes. Not the dancing in a dragon's breath part though. Just the fields of lava and rolling balls of flames traveling windswept tundra's, burning everything in sight."

"Well, just like the mortal realm, we have areas that are different. Our lava plains are to the south, but most of the realm is like this, ranging from colder to much hotter."

"Colder?"

"Yes, we have ice planes too, where instead of stone beneath your feet, its fields of ice."

"Really? I had no idea."

"It's not well known, and those that dare to travel here usually come to this market. It's the most neutral and the safest for humans…" His eyes flick to a pair of elves walking past them, "or rather mortals, I suppose."

"You know I have magic and can protect myself. I am not like most humans."

"Yes, I realize you are a witch because your profile stated as much, but I have not seen you use it. I have met a variety of witches, and their powers vary from very little to powerful. I do not know where you stand on that spectrum, Zadie."

A child-demon pickpocket tries to swipe something from Zadie, shrieks when her wards flare, and runs off smoking.

"All you have to do is ask." Zadie feels her wards flare, her gaze scanning the surrounding crowd, seeing the trail of smoke weaving through the market crowds.

"Then I am asking. What powers do you have? Besides blowing up ex's with a kiss and somehow killing two others." He sends a look toward the child racing away, smoke billowing out behind them. "And apparently burning children."

Zadie side-eyes him, shaking her head. "That's evil, and that was not me. It's the curse tied to me. As for the child, they tried to steal from me. Thieves get burned."

"You're right. That was uncalled for." He holds his hand out. "Come, if I am to see your magic, we should go to the dome."

"The dome?"

"Yes, it's contained, and I can see what you can do."

"Can we not walk there?" She eyes his hand warily and glances around the market.

"No. But I will phase us before we can do damage."

Taking a deep breath, she holds it for a moment before letting it out slowly. Reaching for Zevran, her fingers brush his hand and the instant they touch, his magic wraps around her, tugging her from the market into the heart of an oval arena. Shimmering magic covers them like a blanket of energy, protecting them from the outside world.

Wooden walls ring the space, lined with strange scarecrow-like figures clad in mismatched armor, clutching weapons that range from wicked axes to crackling spell-books. High above, tiered benches rise as in an ancient Roman coliseum, silent witnesses to the training below.

The ground under her boots is the same smooth black stone as the market, cold and unyielding. Her gaze catches on a demon at the far end, muscles rippling as it swings a massive axe at the dummy only to have the target strike back, blow for blow, with uncanny precision. "What is this place?"

"A safe place to train."

"I see that. How does it work?"

"The training dummies react to the power being directed at them." He gestures to one of them and walks over. Creating a ball of fire, he launches it at the dummy, engulfing it. The figure springs to life, gathers the fire into it, and returns it to Zevran, who catches it, and extinguishes it.

"Cute. So it will attack me back."

"Yes, with your own magic, but it's not meant to hurt you. Not in this dome anyway. It's the beginners' dome."

She nods towards the demon near the end. "He doesn't look like a beginner."

"He's not. He's a member of the Royal Guard. The domes range in power from one to five. This is for beginners, so level one. Just because it's level one, does not mean level one in skill. The dummies will react with your skill level, whatever it may be. The key thing is the return magic, or attacks will harm no one. It's for those who wish to practice safely, without damage. Level two adds a bit of damage, enough to make you ache."

Zevran gestures to the other occupant. "Because he needs to be in top form, it would not be good for him to get injured in training, so most on-duty guards practice here. Each gradually increases in power to five, which can kill you if you are not on the ball. Not that we can die permanently. We just return feeling broken for a few days. Levels three and four are where the gambling rings happen. Enough to knock opponents out but not enough to kill."

"And are the other levels here?" Her eyes critically eyed all the figures around the room.

"No, it's a different dome."

"I see. So this will counter what I do?"

"Well, the one with a spell-book will."

"Alright then. Let's do it."

"Do you need your book?"

Zadie laughs. "I am a witch, not a wizard who needs them to cast. I suppose we are a blend of both wizards and sorcerers. If working or creating a new spell, yes, we write it in our book of shadows, but the ones we have learned and practiced are already in our minds and we can recall them at will. Some need components, though, which we carry with us." She wanders over to one holding a spell-book and murmurs a few words. A sparkling shield surrounds her as she chants again, calling forward a wave of magic, sending it into the dummy. She weaves her hands as daggers appear, each following the wave and striking the target.

The dummy retaliates, its spell-book snapping open as it hurls her own magic back at her. Zadie flicks her fingers, sending the attack ricocheting harmlessly off her shield, turning the spell into ice. She spins, drives her heel into it, and grins as the magic shatters into shards. She motions upward, grasping the piece of ice floating from the ground, tilting it to catch her conjured daggers within.

Murmuring another chant, she holds her palm out, her fingers tapping with her thumb, sending a crackle of lightning arcing towards the target, and bouncing to the next one. A grin tips her lips as the second one joins the fray.

"Zadie. That's..." Zevran's voice catches; equal parts amusement and warning.

She winks at him and unleashes a volley of spells at the second dummy while still deflecting the first's counterattacks. She draws a rune in the air and floats it forward, stopping it between them, where it hovers. Seconds later, two waves of energy spill from it, locking the targets in prisons of ice.

Zevran's lips curve, not in the slow, taunting smile she's come to expect, but something more dangerous. "Remind me never to get on the wrong side of you."

She turns, offering a slight bow towards him. "Am I ready for level two?"

Before Zevran can answer, another replies from behind her. "Perhaps level three or four. I would gamble my wages on you."

Zadie spins, her eyes locking on the demon who was fighting earlier, axe casually slung over his shoulder, standing much closer than before. Nearly as tall as Zevran but leaner and clearly all muscle. Dressed in soft red suede pants, combative boots and shirtless. She steps back, feeling Zevran's protective presence stepping in close but not touching her. "Thank you, I think."

Chapter Six

Ashen-Guards

"**Z**adie, this is Mordek from the Ashen-Guards. Mordek, Zadie, my mate. As you can see, I asked her to demonstrate her magical abilities."

"Prince Zevran. Princess Zadie." He offers a slight bow to each of them.

"Prin.... Oh no, I am not... I am just a witch... Human even! It's just Zadie! No titles or anything." Zadie stumbles over her words, her heart suddenly beating faster as her skin pales at the implication of what dating Zevran actually means.

"You are not just a witch. Most of the witches I know cannot cast magic like that. I could feel the power hidden within it from where I was fighting. Hell, even my training dummy reacted to it. It is not surprising that Prince Zevran has you as his mate."

"What's that supposed to mean?"

"Your power. It matches his. I wondered when I saw him here with you. He does not..."

"Enough, Mordek."

Zadie shifts her position to face Zevran, her hands automatically settling on her hips at his expression, reading the warning in his blazing eyes. "Enough why? Is there something you don't want me to know, because if there is, tell me now."

"No, it's nothing." Zevran replies.

"It's clearly something. Is he going to tell me you're a playboy? You know that I have access to the supernatural web and have read stories of the antics of Hell's sons."

Mordek chuckles, reading the challenge in her posture. "I like her; she's feisty. As for Zev here, it's quite the opposite, actually. Some of us were taking bets if he even liked women."

"Mordek..."

Zadie spins back to face Mordek, curiosity eating at her. "Really?"

"Yes, really."

"But what about the stories of the playboy with no name?"

"All about his younger brother Talaris. He's a womanizer, and 90% of the tabloids are all about him, despite the paparazzi seeking other targets in the royal family. They don't dare say his name, or the King would have their heads. So they try to spin it as all of his sons rather than just one."

Zevran huffs. "Mordek, a little forthcoming about the family, aren't you?"

"Shhh, shush, Zev. I want to know." She tests out the nickname, deciding that she prefers his full name, as she slides her gaze his way momentarily, before returning her attention to Mordek. "So Zevran and woman? Tell me!"

"It's not like she's not going to find out by dating you. Demons talk, and some will confront her." He turns back to Zadie. "The last time he spent time with a woman, other than his sisters, was about two hundred years ago, I believe."

"Two hundred... What?" Zadie's mouth falls open, before she snaps it shut, gritting her teeth at not asking the right questions on their first date - not that it lasted long enough to. She clearly needs to make a list of questions to ask next time they get alone time together, pausing in her thoughts as she realizes that she actually wants a next time.

Seeing her discomfort, Mordek grins. "For us, that's barely a long weekend."

She turns toward Zevran, lifting her gaze to his, feeling herself instantly drawn towards the copper depths. "And how old are you exactly?"

His lips curve into a smirk, reading the change in Zadie's body. "Old enough to have ruled kingdoms. Young enough to outlast you in bed."

Zadie rolls her eyes, despite the heat pooling in her core at his words and flushing across her cheeks. "Not an answer."

"Fine, older than you and old enough my dad wants me to get hooked up. Hence joining Supernatural Soulmates."

"I see." She grows silent, pondering what it means for her, as a human, aging, whereas clearly he does not. As a witch, she had magic to slow it down, but not hundreds of years down. How was it possible that she's mated to practically an immortal? "So why not just choose from one of the demons? Why Supernatural Soulmates?"

"Because none of them appealed to me, Zadie. I have lived long enough to have met most of them. I wanted something different."

Mordek watches, feeling the energy bouncing between them. "Speaking of hooked up, your father is throwing a ball tonight in your honor. It starts in an hour."

"Wait. What? Since when?"

"Since he heard you had a date with a human. Apparently he's invited all the single female demons and intends to pick one for you."

Zevran's jaw ticks slightly, his eyes blazing with heat at Mordek's words. Clenching his fists, he growls out. "He is not picking for me. I have a mate!"

Mordek steps back, holding his hands up protectively. "Hey! I realize that. I just wanted to warn you in case you are planning on introducing her. You are walking into a lion's den and should be prepared."

"How did he even find out?"

"Apparently, Veyra is responsible for the little date tidbit making it to your father."

Growling, he forces himself to calm down. "Well, I guess Daddy Dearest is in for a surprise because I am NOT taking a demon as a bride."

Zadie shudders inside at Mordek's words, keeping an outward stance of calm. Zevran's father hasn't met her and already thinks she's not good enough for his son because she's human. A lesser being of his ilk. How is she supposed to compare to the others? Suddenly feeling ill, she murmurs quietly. "We don't need to see him today. I am not even dressed for a ball."

"Yes, we do, and your dress is perfect for it. All the more reason to walk in there as if you own the place. If anyone says anything out of line to you, I give you full permission to destroy them with your power. In fact, I hope one of them does, because it will show him you can stand all on your own here in Hell."

"No, I am just a..."

Mordek interrupts her. "He's right. Your power matches the royal line and its guards. There would be few in our realm you could not take. And it's not like they are going to die, really."

"So I have heard... But what if I am arrested, or marked as an outcast because of it. Then you would be forced to live in my realm."

"Zadie. My father values power above all else, and that's what he will see. He will not arrest you because I won't let him. If he banishes you, then he banishes me, and he won't risk that."

Mordek chuckles. "If he does, then he will banish some of the Ashen-Guards with him, because we are sworn to protect the prince. I highly doubt he wants to train more."

Zadie glances between the two. "But Zevran doesn't travel with guards."

"He does, you just can't see us. We excel at remaining unseen."

"Like blending into the crowds? I am pretty certain he was alone in the coffee shop."

"Nope. The King would have our heads if we left him alone... or if he found out."

"The coffee shop was not big enough for you to be hiding."

"You would think, but there is a reason we are called Ashen-Guards." Mordek's body breaks apart into tiny motes of ash, before they fade from her view, leaving only red eyes staring at her. He winks, then disappears completely, shifting around her to appear on the other side, showing only his eyes.

"That's not invisibility because I can see creatures with that skill. What is it?"

Mordek reforms beside her with a smirk. "Phase walking. Not in your realm but not in another. Think of it as a mirror realm or the in-between. When we are there watching, we see you, but everything is reflected. Something we train for because our reactions go for what we see, not what's really there."

Zadie smiles, trying to recall if she had seen any eyes in the coffee shop, but finally admits defeat. "I did not see you."

"No, you had eyes only for the Prince."

"Well, now I am going to watch for you."

"Have you seen the other two lurking?"

"What?"

"Thane, Nicx, you may show yourselves." Zevran chuckles, watching his two guards appear about thirty feet away, one on either side of him. "These three are part of what I call the Doom Dorks! We grew up together, along with Pyrrh and Skarix, who are off duty right now. Thane is on my left. Nicx on my right. They are what you consider friends, despite my father telling us all..." He stiffens his shoulders and puffs out his chest, pretending to adjust an invisible crown before pointing at the group, clearly mimicking his father. "You are the crown prince, and with that comes specific obligations. They are your guards and not to be befriended. Treat them as such!"

Thane and Nicx approach, each offering a subtle bow towards Zevran. "Greetings Zadie. May we call you that? We are better known as his babysitters, but we would never tell Daddy Dearest that."

Zevran glances around and flicks his fingers as if dismissing them. "Alright, enough formality. I do not sense anyone watching."

The three laugh together. "Would you care if he were?"

Zevran chuckles. "No, I wouldn't, but I know you do."

"It's our jobs on the line, not yours."

"Right, like I would let him fire you."

"Perhaps we can all move above ground. Buy a big house!"

Zevran shakes his head. "If I move above ground, you get your own house. Besides, we have a house above ground you can move into."

"Nope, sorry, no can do. I mean, how would we protect you?"

"Fine, a separate suite then."

"That we can do. So what about you, Zadie? Are you moving in?" Mordek asks.

"Oh no, I have a cottage."

"Right now you do, but what if you and Zevran make it official? What then?"

Zadie stops and stares at Mordek, uncertain how to answer that since she hasn't gotten past the whole killing him part.

Zevran growls softly. "Alright. Enough. It's not something we have discussed, so don't push her. Now, we should probably head to the castle."

Chapter Seven

Charognis

"Before you do, you should know Daddy brought out Charognis. He sensed your mortal entering." Mordek informs them.

"What?"

"Charognis is a dog, right?" Zadie asks.

"Yes. He should have greeted you before we got here, but being a prince, I know ways past him."

"Why would he have greeted me? Why would your father do that?"

"He's the one that prevents the dead from leaving and the living from entering without permission. And you, my dear, are here without his knowledge. Granted, you had my permission, so there is that." Zevran replies.

"What's he going to do to me?"

"Nothing. He will report back to my father that you are here with me. Just show no fear."

"Got it. Anything else I should know?"

"Other than his three heads, snakes protruding from the mane around his neck and a serpent for a tail, no. He's really a softy in disguise."

"Right, the three-headed, snake-ridden guard dog of Hell is a softy."

Zevran chuckles and gestures to the path before them. "Come; if we walk, it will take us about thirty minutes. Are you good with that?"

"Yes, it will give me more time to see your realm."

The two of them stroll alongside each other, neither touching but each feeling the draw to the other, shifting just a little closer. As they near the stone walls surrounding the castle, an oversized dog bounds out of the ironwoods. It stalks forward, its crimson eyes locked on Zadie, teeth bared on all three of its heads.

Zadie freezes, her gaze darting over to Zevran momentarily. She takes a deep breath and straightens her shoulders, turning to face the dog and holding her hand out, palm up. She lifts her gaze up to his, feeling each of the heads' hot breath on her skin as he sniffs over her.

"Charognis, that's enough. She's with me. You didn't fail in your duties. I brought her." Zevran says.

Charognis grumbles in a deep voice. "All mortals through me, Princeling. You know the rules."

"Yes, well, this one's my mate. She gets a pass."

Charognis steps back and plants his butt down, tilting his middle head sideways, while the others watch Zadie intently. "Are you sure?"

"Yes. The whole sparks when we touch. The pull on my soul and the desire to be closer. Plus, she's cursed, just like me, so we are perfect."

"In what way?"

"I don't know the origins of her curse, but she has killed three of her past boyfriends with it."

Charognis chuckles, offering a paw over to Zadie. "Welcome to Hell."

Zadie unfreezes and raises her hand, shaking his paw gently. "Thank you."

"Are you heading to the castle?"

"I believe so," Zadie replies.

"Have fun, pretty mate." He stands and shakes himself, bounding back into the woods he came from.

Chapter Eight

Hellfire Gardens

Zadie breathes a sigh of relief as the dog bounds back into the woods, turning to Zevran. "Well, that was fun."

"It was, wasn't it? Let's make some more trouble!" Zevran leads her along a wide obsidian causeway, polished so smooth it reflects the light of the blue Hellfire torches that line the path. He pauses at a pair of dark iron gates, bars twisted into barbed spirals resembling both roses and thorns, waiting as they glide open silently. Stepping through, he pauses, his eyes drifting to Zadie, who stops beside him, looking around in awe.

Statues of fallen angels, wings broken but heads held proud, their eyes reflecting the molten lava spilling from the fountains they stand upon. Instead of falling into a pool, they spread outward in the basin, creating a geometric design, before disappearing at the edges into unknown depths. Surrounding the edges are granite beds of blood-red roses entwined with blackened screaming nightshades. Scattered among the planters stand obsidian trees, whose leaves reflect the crimson clouds and silent lightning in the sky above, like red stained glass.

Beyond that, the dark stone castle looms, its turrets clawing skyward with jagged points instead of the neat, squared battlements of mortal keeps. The walls pulse with etched wards, glowing like veins of fire, endlessly shifting and rearranging so no intruder can ever map them. Amber light flickers in the rows of arched windows cut into the stone, as unseen creatures move within.

Hellhounds prowl in the shadows, their eyes like embers as they weave through the demons milling around, growling at any that get too close. Noticing the various styles of dress on the demons, ranging from nearly naked to ballgowns that would rival the rich and famous, she glances his way and asks. "Is it always like this?"

"When my father is having a party? Yes. The ballroom is around the corner, its doors opening out onto the courtyard. This way, no one is in the inner sanctum. Only the outer wards." He leans in and whispers in her ear. "See, your dress is the best of all of them here."

Zadie blushes and looks away from the crowd. "I don't know; there are some pretty extravagant gowns over there."

"I do. Come, let's do a tour of the private gardens before I take you into the main hall." He reaches for her, watching her pull away from his touch. "Zadie..."

"No, it's bad enough in my realm and then there is what happened in the market. I don't know what will happen here at your castle."

Zevran nods and gestures to the left side of the castle, where another set of gates wait. This one, rather than being welded into vertical bars, is instead three roses; its thorny stems leading into a vase beneath them. He runs his fingers over the roses, and down to the thorns, pricking one with his finger. The blood slithers down the stem into the pot at the base. Each rose flickers once, and the gates swing open.

"Blood magic?"

"Yes, only the royal family can open this gate."

"Unless someone has a drop of your blood."

"There is that, but few know about it. They just know the gate stays closed and they can't even hop over it. The only way into these gardens is through opening the gate."

"And yet, there are demons that lurk in the shadows, who could be watching. I mean, there *is* a ball going on."

"True. If they watched me, they would see me caress the stem, not the blood. If they make it past this gate, there are guards around to stop them from going any further." He guides her in and waits until the gate swings closed behind them, leading her down a cobblestone path. On either side, a variety of unknown plants sway and murmur in lost tongues, some reaching for Zevran as he walks past.

Zadie stops and stares at the gardens. "I have never seen such plants. What are they?"

"Variants of the nightshade family and... bloodthorn roses, ash lilies, widow's bloom, plus a few cinderblooms for ambiance. Do not touch the vines; they're always hungry."

"Which ones are which?"

"Is that you, or your witch's side asking?"

"Both."

Chuckling, he points out the flowers as they walk by. "These are bloodthorn roses; the petals drip blood instead of dew in the morning. They feed off the pain of those around. The more in pain, the better the bloom. Scattered throughout them all are what's known as red hostas. They are large black leaves with red veins that look like fire, our grounding plant."

"Grounding how?"

"Some of these plants exude magical energy. Hostas absorb them and stop the magic from mixing. The more they absorb, the redder the center. That way the gardener knows to plant more because they should be mostly black."

They wander over to a bed of pale flowers with ashen-grey leaves, its edges glowing faintly. "These are ash lilies. They thrive in fire, releasing a smoke that induces visions. Seers and oracles pay handsomely for them."

Moving further down the path, he leads her around to a small courtyard. In the center, a round planter rises from the cobblestone. Inside are jet black orchids, each of its petals lined with a single red vein, giving it a sinister look. As Zadie steps forward, Zevran shakes his head and places an arm out to block her. "No, that flower is known as a widow's bloom. Not for mortals. Just breathing in its scent will evoke mind-crippling memories of lost lovers, something I am certain you do not want, considering one of them imploded."

Zadie nods and backs up a step. "Why do you have them?"

"Because they are only harmful to mortals. Demons who have lost loved ones, use them to bring them back in their mind."

"Wait, I thought you couldn't be killed?"

"Not in your realm and not really here. There are some magics that will do it, but most of those seeking these flowers are ones that have died from old age."

"I see. So its another vision-inducing flower?"

"Yes, but this one is very specific. Ash lilies are not. They help with all visions, and you never know what you will see."

"So much like magic mushrooms then."

"Yes, if that is the human equivalent."

"I suspect it is." Her eyes stray to the flowers again. "They are quite beautiful. I have always loved lilies."

"Good to know." Veering to the left, he takes a path hidden beyond a clinging vine, with glowing red thorns that curl and uncurl like hungry mouths, hissing as they walk by.

Zadie stops and stares at them, finding they remind her of the nightshade sitting in her kitchen. "Are they like the nightshades?"

"In a way. These are ebonfire vines. They are not part of the nightshade family, but they bite the same."

"I think the nightshades are quite sweet." She reaches out to them, only to flinch as Zevran grasps her hand and pulls it away. Her eyes shift to the nearby statue, watching a few pieces break and fall from it as thunder booms across the sky.

"They are not sweet, and they will bite."

"Says you." Zadie huffs, giving an apologetic look to the plant.

"Perhaps someplace safer. First, we need to pass the soul-eater's poppy."

"Oh, those sound safe." Rolling her eyes, Zadie follows, seeing a few plants she recognizes, specifically the belladonna family. She hesitates at one, admiring the purple-black blossom, wondering if she can snip a sprout and grow it in her garden.

"It is as long as you don't breathe in its scent. It steals fragments of memories and happiness."

"What, so I am supposed to hold my breath in a garden that is full of scents?"

Zevran chuckles. "No, just don't stuff your nose in the blooms and inhale like a lot of mortals seem to do."

"Noted."

As they weave through the pathways, Zevran leads her onto a trellised walkway.

Tiny orange flowers spark between the green leaves, like a tiny flint trying to ignite its tinder. "What are these?"

"Cinderbloom. They grow wild all over the realm, much like weeds in yours. The children love them."

"Why?"

"Touch one."

"What, you are letting me touch the plants now?"

"Only this one."

She narrows her eyes at him, suspecting a trick, but then he did state kids loved them, so they couldn't be that bad, could they? Hesitantly, she reaches out and touches the closest flower, flinching as a small display of fireworks erupts from it. Seconds later, the flower re-blooms, spreading its petals out once more. "That was amazing." Her fingers move to a nearby one, the effect mimicking the first, but with slightly different colors. "I can see why. I love them too."

"I see caution is taking over." Laughing, Zevran takes his hand and sweeps it along the trellis, creating a cascade of light surrounding him, pausing and then sweeping it back to the same effect. "They react and come back instantly. Over and over. Hours of fun."

Zadie giggles and sweeps her hands over it like Zevran has, spinning beneath the display of fireworks. "I want these in my backyard!"

"Alas, they only grow in Hell. Others have tried but were unsuccessful."

"Damn."

"You can take a snipping later tonight if you wish, after I introduce you to my father."

Zadie nods, her eyes straying to a patch of nightshades as she wanders over, watching them sway and hiss at her presence. "Is there anything that nightshades need, nutrient wise?"

"Why do you ask?" Zevran moves up to stand beside her.

"Because I planted the ones you gave me."

"You did what?"

"Well yes. They like sweet milk... a lot actually, but I was wondering if they need anything, like calcium, which prevents blossom rot on tomatoes. Or coffee grinds to add nitrogen, making the soil slightly acidic for the plants that need that. I put mulched banana peels, which adds potassium, to help with flowering on some of my rarer varieties of herbs. That sort of thing."

Zevran stares at her, reading the honesty in her questioning. "You're serious?"

"Well yes. You gave them to me; I want to keep them alive."

"Right then. The gardeners usually tend them, but I know they like crushed charred bones because if we ever find any, we dump them here as per the gardeners' request."

"Like I have those lying around." She rolls her eyes at his comment.

"I am not a gardener, Zadie. I just enjoy the flowers and picked some for you. When I see him next, I will ask. How's that?"

She mumbles under her breath. "I knew it."

"Knew what?"

"That you don't seem like the gardening type. The supernatural web doesn't tell me because they *only grow* in the royal gardens." She lifts her fingers and air quotes in annoyance. "Met with an internet wall of *it's a closely guarded secret...* no matter where I searched."

"Well, despite being a royal secret, they are now growing elsewhere. Most would not dare to plant nightshades."

"Well, as I said, I was not letting them die."

Zevran nods, finding himself intrigued even more at the woman that would dare to plant something that would rip her fingers off. "Come, I should take you inside to meet my father." He guides her through the rest of the gardens, catching her glances to the nightshades every time they pass a batch.

As they near the back door, Zadie hesitates, her gaze drifting out to the glistening black on the horizon. "What is that?"

"The black river."

"Can we..."

"No. The river's surface is a mirror, currently reflecting the light from the night sky. You can see it from a distance, but if you get too close, it shows what you fear the most and brings it to life. Even demons do not stray near it. That is why Father had the castle built here, because few will cross its waters. He only has to worry about assaults from the front doors since it wraps around three quarters of this castle."

"Does that actually happen? Like demons attacking the castle?"

"Not really. The occasional angry soul does, but they are taken down pretty quickly. Centuries ago, during the Demon Wars, yes. There was also a red dragon that took out half the castle. Dad was less than impressed that he had to rebuild, but it's been quiet of late."

Pushing the door in, he steps in to hold it open, waiting as she steps inside with him. Once she's in, he closes it and leads her down a torch-lit hallway. The dark obsidian walls reflect the dancing flames, making it look as though they are walking through a tunnel of flames. Her chunky heels thud gently on the jasper floors, its blood-red coloration laced with darker swirls, giving her the impression of congealed flame.

Chapter Nine

Daddy Dearest

Zevran watches Zadie walk through the hallway, seeing her eyes dart all around her as she takes in his castle. A place he grew up in and something he takes for granted. Looking at it in a new light, he can imagine how impressive it would be, but for him, it is just home.

Pushing open heavy stone doors, he steps into the ballroom and looks around, seeing a lot of the usuals; each dancing in gowns that smoke at the hems, or suits embroidered in molten gold. Knowing they are here, not just to honor his father, but to remind everyone else that they belong here; that their names carry weight, and their whispers can ruin you.

Zadie steps in beside him, her eyes doing a sweep of the room, hearing the laughter and reading it for what it is: darkness, cunning, hidden behind the veneer of caring. Some guests fawn over the man himself, perched on a throne with two crossed blades sunk into three skulls apiece looming behind him. A black runner spills out from his feet, unfurling down the center of the ballroom, covering the jasper beneath their feet. Colored torches flicker and dance, their light scattering across the stone wall and the shimmering dresses of the guests. "Who needs a disco ball when you have this?" She mutters softly under her breath.

"Do not be lured by the facade you see before you, Zadie." Zevran closes the door behind them. "They are demons."

"So are you?"

"True, but not all have the honor that was bred into us by our father. Some of them will happily slit your throat without a second thought."

"So he has honor then?"

"Perhaps that's not the right word. He rules Hell and has earned the respect of most of the souls down here. Just because they won't stab him in the back, doesn't mean they won't stab their friends in the back if it will better their position with him. If that makes sense."

"And what about you?"

"I am a demon, Zadie. Next in line to rule, but I would never betray you, or the relationship we might have."

She lifts her gaze to his momentarily, giving a nod. "So, who's here that I need to be aware of besides your father?"

"Don't worry. From what I can see, it's the usual crowd." His eyes flick over the crowd, cataloguing faces he'd long since grown tired of. "House Algonod. Otherwise known as Dukes of Desire." He points to the back corner where a group of velvet-clad residents lie draped across their lounge chairs, their gold jewelry glinting in the light. Each is strikingly handsome in their own way. "If they haven't seduced someone by midnight, they'll start bribing them instead."

A flash of steel catches his gaze as he leads Zadie further in, commenting on those they pass. "Ah, Trezzek's war dogs. I see they polished their blades just for the occasion. Subtle as always. They are war-born nobles who pride themselves on their armies and dueling prowess."

A veiled woman glides by, the scent of roses and ash trailing her. Zevran's smile thins. "Lady Seraphine Netherax. Stunning, elegant, and rumored to have buried six husbands; none of which were natural deaths. If she asks you to dance, run."

Zadie's eyes trail over the woman, immediately noticing the coldness in the woman's eyes, as she smiles Zevran's way, followed by the distaste as she skims her gaze over to Zadie, catching the ever so slight. "Ugh, mortal."

Across the ballroom, fireworks spark in the air above a man laughing too loudly. "Lord Veyric Cindral. If he doesn't set the drapes on fire by the end of the night, I'll be shocked. It's a good thing Father makes him leave his fire-breathing horses outside the castle grounds."

He gestured discreetly toward a cluster of black-clad figures whispering in a corner. "House Tagrech, the Keepers of Secrets. Don't stare too long, or you'll end up cursed with boils or bad luck in bed." He leans in and whispers in her ear. "And we wouldn't want that, now would we, my darling mate."

Zadie blushes at his words, averting her gaze over to a group of three in the corner. Also dressed in extravagant silk, they stand not much taller than her and are squabbling over who has the sharper horns.

Zevran sighs at what's drawn her attention. "The Triune of Spite. The three of them always travel together, despite their constant bickering. Gnats. Loud, pompous, and impossible to squash without Father noticing."

His gaze snags on a too-familiar smirk across the room. His jaw tightens and ticks as he grits his teeth, stepping in closer to Zadie. "And of course, Lord Xorgol of the Eastern Hemisphere. My favorite reminder is that even Hell has pests who think they're charming. If he smirks at me one more time, I may just introduce his face to the floor."

Zadie laughs at the apparent jealousy, daring to nudge him gently, feeling the current flow through the room at their touch. Thunder rumbles outside, blending with the screaming nightshade, sensing the chaos powers within. Her gaze drifts to the open ballroom doors, seeing a few more demons filtering in. "How many times till he's exalted with the floor?"

"Excuse me?"

"My friend Nim plays video games and always jokes that she's exalted with the floor as if it's an actual reputation. Meaning her character dies often. There are several tiers they have to go through: four, I think, but I am uncertain."

"I see." Zevran's brows furrow, his hand lifting to rub his chin.

Zadie laughs at his confused expression. "Clearly, you don't know, and it's okay. I don't claim to understand either, but she loves the game."

"You're right. I don't." He chuckles, letting his gaze sweep over the demons in the room. "Behind my father sit three of my siblings. The ones he actually managed to wrangle into showing up. Talaris, the one the tabloids love. Probably here to get on fathers good side. Then Rurik and Kharen. They're the youngest, which explains why they're here instead of off causing their own chaos like the rest of us. And that's it. The ones who matter, anyway. Congratulations, you've officially met Hell's nobility."

"Not all of it." Her eyes shift to the throne at the end, meeting the narrowed gaze of Zevran's father.

"Yes, well, I suppose we should get that over with." He places a hand beneath her elbow and starts to lead her forward, before removing it quickly. His attention darts to the drapery along the side, flapping as a wind billows through them, followed by the scream of the nightshades outside, overriding the sound of something cracking from somewhere in the castle. "Father. This is Zadie. She's my mate. Zadie, this is my father, the Sovereign King of the Underworld, Draemorr."

"She's human."

"How very astute of you, Father."

"Get rid of her." He waves his hand and picks up the goblet on his left, taking a sip.

Zevran stiffens at his father's words. "I am not getting rid of her. She's my mate. You demanded that I join the dating app. I did. You pushed me to date when I didn't want to. I did. You want me to marry and settle down because it's *time*. She's my choice because she's my mate. I am not settling for anything less."

"You will marry a demon. Not a pathetic human."

Zadie's eyes flash in anger. "Pathetic? You do not know who I am to even make that judgement!"

"I don't need to. I can smell the reek of mortal blood in your veins. Guards, take her out of here."

Zevran growls, drawing the attention of the ballroom back to the throne, as two guards approach. "Do not touch her."

"What's the matter, son? Worried about your chosen bride? Mortals are weak, and this is just proof. You will always need to defend her. There are plenty of worthy demons out there, like Veyra." Draemorr gestures to the guards again, his eyes flicking over her in disdain.

Zadie reaches out and places a hand on Zevran's arm, seeing the skulls crack behind him as a mirror shatters elsewhere in the room, earning a few hisses from the nearby demons shifting away from the falling shards. "I would like to see them try to touch me."

"Dad, enough! I don't like Veyra, and I certainly don't want to be tied to the Baelgrith household." Zevran covers her hand with his, the nightshades screaming outside now drowning out the murmur of conversation in the ballroom. "Your demand was that I choose someone to settle down with. I have! Zadie is my mate!"

Draemorr sighs and lifts a hand, flicking his fingers. A small bead of light streams towards Zadie, expanding into a ball of fire.

Narrowing her eyes, Zadie curses under her breath, feeling the magic in the room before it appears. Reacting, she draws a quick symbol in the air in front of her, watching as the ball of fire launches her way. She weaves another set of letters into the rune quickly, just as the ball strikes it. She smiles as it bounces harmlessly off her and back at his father, engulfing him in his own flames, burning through his clothing and baring his chest for all to see. Her eyes stray over the tattoos on his skin, landing on the prominent one of barbed wire wrapped around a crown. Shifting her gaze over to Zevran, she wonders if he has any, and finds she wants to rip the shirt off to find out.

Draemorr stands immediately, brushing away the flaming remnants of his clothing, turning his wrath Zadie's way. "She's a bloody witch?"

"Yes, she is, and you just tried to kill her." Zevran's eyes shift, his irises darkening to blood red as claws elongate from the tips of his fingers, taking a menacing step forward.

Mordek materializes beside him, grasping his arm. "Zevran. It's your father. Don't."

"Son! I did what I thought was best. Demons have longer lives than mortals. They are better suited to be your bride."

"No, you just don't like that I chose your most hated race. Too bad Dad. Zadie is the only one I will accept."

"Don't touch me!" Zadie spins as Draemorr's two guards reach out to grasp her arms. She twists her hand, calling forth a wave of force that slams into them and flings them into the crowds now avidly watching. She draws a rune in the air and flicks it towards them, encasing both of them in ice. "Anyone else want to test me? Because I am about done with this world. Zevran, take me home. Your father is a pompous asshole."

Zevran grasps her hand and pulls her in close, hearing something crash above them in the castle, as a wind buffets through the ballroom. "Thanks for the support... Dad..."

"Son, wait. Let's talk about this."

"Talk about what? That she's a powerful witch who can defeat your guards. Is she good enough now? Too bad that's not good enough for me." He shimmers and pulls Zadie from the room, bringing her back to her front door. Once they are safe, he releases her and steps away, feeling the energies calm around them. "Sorry, I thought my father would be more accepting of my choice."

Zadie shakes her head and steps back against her door, her hand moving to the knob and twisting it. "It's fine. Thank you for the tour. Your gardens were lovely, but I think I need some space."

"Zadie, please. Don't give up on us."

"I just can't right now." She opens the door and slips through it, closing and locking it after her. She leans against it, feeling his presence step up to the door, and waits... waits for the handle to turn beside her, to see if he is daring enough step into her domain.

Zevran places his palm against the wood, caressing it as if the door were not standing between them. "I love you, Zadie. I will not let you go that easily." With that, he shimmers away, landing on a desolate mountain edge, where he sits down to think.

Zadie pulls away from the door, her eyes darting to the nightshade in the kitchen as she passes, and pads into her bedroom. There she strips and dumps her clothing on the floor. Pulling on an oversized T-shirt, she crawls into bed and hugs a pillow to her chest. Feeling Soot jump on the mattress, she shakes her head. "I don't want to talk about it."

"Alright, Zadie." He curls up against her, purring softly.

Zadie switches the pillow out, burrowing her face in his fur as tears slip from her eyes, her heart breaking inside at what happened until sleep eventually takes her.

Chapter Ten

Scandel

The next morning, Zadie pads into the kitchen, still half-asleep, following the call of morning tea. As she fills the machine and waits for it to percolate the hot water into the pot, she turns her attention to the nightshade basking in the morning sun. "Good morning, little Beastlies," she murmurs, brushing her fingers across the velvety petals.

The plants answer with soft, leafy hisses, each petal leaning toward her hand like cats competing for attention. She laughs softly. "Yes, yes, I'll pet you all. No favoritism here." She works her way along the pot, inspecting the new leaves and tracing her fingers over each stem, noticing each one is about a third larger than when she planted them.

"Hmm... Is that pot going to be big enough? I might have to hit the hardware store. Or suppose I could search online about your growth rate, but you're a closely guarded secret of the royal garden's, aren't you? Can't exactly post a question about the mystical nightshade without someone knocking on my door."

"You could always ask Zevran."

"I did." Zadie glances over as Soot strolls in, tail flicking lazily before he leaps onto the counter, prowling over to her side.

The nightshades respond with a chorus of shrill piercing screams, their stems instantly bristling with thorny spikes.

"Hey now! Stop that racket! Do you want to wake the entire forest?" She covers her ears and glares at the potted flowers. "We are not playing this game in my house. I figured out you were temperamental last night at the ball, but that doesn't mean it can happen here. Soot is my familiar, which means he's off-limits, and you can put those weapons away or I will stick you outside with the other plants."

The hissing softens to a sulky whisper as the spikes withdraw within the soft rustle of leaves.

"That's better," she mutters, pouring her tea. "Honestly, it's like having children with anger management issues. I guess that's why you earned your name, screaming nightshades. It's enough to rupture an eardrum."

"And did he know?" Soot asks.

She glances at Soot. "No, other than telling me they drop the crushed remains of charred bones on them. He was going to ask his gardener."

"Yes, that seems about right. A lot of Hellish plants need things like that. The ashes of burned contracts, remnants of broken souls, that sort of thing." Soot smirks, well, as much as a cat can, and bats one of the folded leaves, earning a hiss from the plants.

"Soot. Leave them alone. You know better."

"Do I though?"

"Yes, you do." Zadie mutters as she lifts her cup and pads into the living room. "Great. Tea and a turf war."

Soot jumps off the counter and follows her into the living room. "When are you seeing him again?"

"I don't know if I should after yesterday. Daddy clearly did NOT approve of our relationship. Besides, we have made no plans to."

"I see. You should ask him out."

"I am staying in today. I have things to do."

"Like?"

"A list of orders that I have ignored for the past two days."

"Bah, you are a witch. You could have those magically whipped up in seconds. Besides, you did a bunch yesterday. How many are left outstanding?"

"Enough that I don't want to get behind, and you know I enjoy doing them by hand. Stop pushing me, Soot." She moves towards the desk that sits nestled in the corner of the room and places her cup on the coaster. Tucking herself in her chair, she boots the computer up and scrolls through her orders, writing them down on the notepad beside her. Once she's finished, she picks up her cup and sips her tea, shifting over to the Supernatural Soulmates site, wanting to see if Zevran messaged her, but not daring to admit it to Soot. Seeing nothing there, she casually flips through the news, stopping to stare at a headline, as the cup slips from her fingers, and crashes to the ground.

"Damn it." She chants a few words, watching the cup reform and the liquid evaporate. Leaning down, she picks her mug up and sets it carefully on the desk, turning her attention back to the headline.

Swipe Right for Damnation? Hellion Royale's Love Match with Snow Lily Shocks Court.

"How the hell did they get that info? Supernatural Soulmates guaranteed privacy." She scans down, seeing a couple more headlines along the same lines.

Ballroom Inferno! Snow Lily Outsmarts the Sovereign King.
The Witch Who Wouldn't Bow - New Queen in the Making?

Soot jumps up onto the chair with her, placing his front paws on the desk to look at the screen. "Get what?"

Zadie wraps her arms around Soot and plants him in her lap. "Our dating app names."

"Hey, at least it's your dating names and not your real ones. It was likely the oracles, and not the actual dating app. People pay them big bucks to get that kind of information."

"Why would they do that?"

"Would you rather it was your real name? You recall what the press did when Desmond blew up? That's why we moved here, to the middle of bumfuck nowhere!"

"No, but I would think they would know his name since he's first in line to the throne, and he introduced me as Zadie in front of all the guests."

"They do. But Daddy Dearest would probably shred them if they used it. Being the King of Hell has its uses. So to avoid his wrath, they use names everyone knows is the crown prince, but not actually naming him."

"I guess. I wonder why they didn't use mine then."

"Same reason, except this time it would be the Crown Prince after them. So what does it say?"

"Just that we shocked the courts. I didn't open the article."

Soot reads through the page, noticing a mix of headlines. "Some of those, though, are going to cause issues."

"Which ones?"

"The ones questioning the family. The king will shut those down fast." Soot lifts a paw and points to a few on the screen below the one that Zadie stopped at.

Family Feud in Flames! Does War Loom as Heir Defies King Before All of Hell?

Prince's Defiance or True Love? Witch Over Bloodline.

Pomp, Power, and a Pompous Ass: King Draemorr Burned by His Own Fire.

"Damn, now I am really glad they used our app names, especially since I called him a pompous asshole in front of everyone."

"You should be, though I suspect Daddy Dearest is already trying to track you and the reporters for your disrespect."

"Soot! That's not good!"

"You have the cottage warded. I think you are safe. Besides, you have the nightshades in the kitchen. They should react to the infernal presence."

"Right, there is that, and Zevran only gave my first name, not my last one. I am certainly not the only Zadie in the realm."

"Let's hope the oracles keep silent then. Have you been to Hell's Bloggers to see what they say yet?"

"Wait, they have bloggers?"

"Yes, go to the Infernal Insider. The paparazzi post their pictures and blogs there."

"How do you know... Nevermind..."

Soot shrugs and settles on her lap, purring softly. "I told you. I browse a lot when you are busy."

"Fine." She leans in and searches for the website, clicking it open. She gasps in shock at all the headlines and reads through them, shaking her head in dismay.

Witch's Beauty Rocks the Royal Court.

Hellion Royale's New Witch Causes a Stir.

Frozen Solid! Ballroom Guards Humiliated by Mortal Sorceress.

Is Snow Lily the Future Queen of Hell?

Hellion Royale Plucks Snow Lily.

"He didn't pluck me, and I am not a sorceress. I am a witch!! What the hell is this shit?"

"Welcome to the paparazzi of Hell. They love their headlines and stories. This is nothing; the blogs are where it's at. They have the dirt of the underworld."

Zadie shifts the mouse over to the blog tab and clicks it open, her eyes dropping to the first one, apparently written by someone called Petals in the Pit.

Who Is Snow Lily?

So, apparently, our beloved Hellion Royale, Crown Prince of Sulfur and Smoke, showed up at the last Midnight Masquerade with a witch. Not just any witch. One called Snow Lily, alabaster hair and frostbite eyes; dressed like she owned the place. Sources say she didn't flinch when Charognis sniffed her. Some are calling it confidence. Others are calling it a pure death wish. Especially the ballroom brawl of fire, ice, and family drama. Either way, she's officially the most interesting thing to happen to Hell's royal scene since the Molten Wine Incident.

"Soot! No! Just... I can't believe this!"

"Exactly! These are the best!"

"These are NOT the best Soot! Oh, my Gawd!"

"Yes, they are. Look at the next one by the Devil's Whisper. Petal and Poison. It's so you."

She walks in, wearing black silk and molten gold; like the throne room was her runway. He doesn't take his eyes off her. Suddenly, the whispers stop being about her hair or her dress and start being about whether she's the next Queen of Hell; challenging the King himself by returning the fireball meant to end her. Hellion Royale might just be sealing his fate... with a kiss.

"If only they knew what your kisses do!" Soot exclaims.

"Yes, because I had to. You cannot show fear when approaching royalty. And no, NO kiss. That's a guaranteed death for him. Wait, what if they know? Why would that say he is sealing his fate with a kiss if they didn't? I can just imagine the headlines. Snow Lily, the Frost Witch, Freezes Hellion Royale, or Snow Lily's Ice Lips Douse the Crown Prince's Flames. That's just great. Now I am coming up with punchlines for our relationship. What am I going to do?"

"Well, there is space to write your own blog. You could do... From Heat to Hailstorm: Hellion Royale Caught in a Chilling Embrace... Or... Attack the King Again like the Others with Royal Roast: Draemorr Charred. Witch Untouched."

"NO! Whose side are you on, Soot?"

"Well, yours of course, unless there is juicy gossip, then I am on its side. Speaking of which, is it true that he didn't take his eyes off you?"

"I don't know, Soot. I was doing my best to stay upright and not panic."

"Man, I wish I were there, weaving between their legs, listening to their chatter."

"No, you don't." Zadie closes her eyes and leans her head back against the chair. "I did not think it would be this much of a scandal. We should never have gone to the ball and met his father in public. I just want to stay here and forget it ever happened."

"Too late now. Look at it this way; not all the paparazzi were paying attention."

"What do you mean?"

"Little Miss Demon Dish was late to the party. Theirs says insiders tell me, the whole romance started on Supernatural Soulmates, which means Hellion Royale wasn't even looking for royalty-approved brides. Instead, he swiped on a witch known as Snow Lily. The Court is fuming, and not in the fun, brimstone way. If you thought the Succubus Scandal was big, just wait until HR brings her to meet Daddy. Well, you have already met Daddy."

"Yes, and he didn't like me. Zevran had to tell him several times that we were mates, especially when he started pushing lesser demons on him and how they were better than a mere human. Not to discount the fireball he tossed at me and the guards that tried to take me away." Zadie places him aside and rises from the chair, pacing across the room. "I don't know, Soot. Perhaps they all know something I don't. Maybe I am meant to be alone forever."

Soot perches on the chair, his eyes following Zadie's movements. "You are not. Besides, the gossip rags change as quickly as the tides. Some succubus will do something with the wrong person, and they will take over. He is your mate. You owe it to yourselves to see this through."

Zadie's shoulders slump as she sinks down onto the couch, placing her hands on her face. "I am so torn right now, Soot."

Soot jumps off the chair and pads across the room, launching into her lap and purring against her. "Look. Don't think of the gossip, or Daddy, or anyone else. Not even the curse. This is between you and Zevran. What does your heart tell you?"

"That I want to see him again."

"Good. Next question. When did you decide you liked him?"

"On our first date at the coffee shop. When he walked through the door and everyone's gaze turned towards him, I wanted to create a magical wall to stop them from looking or to drag him from the coffee shop. There was just something about him."

"So, date one then."

"What are you getting at, Soot?"

"That you have seen him on three separate occasions, and he's still alive."

"Yes, and?"

"Isn't that when all your humans died? Three dates after you admitted feelings for them."

"Well, technically one week after, and one of those doesn't count. He was dropping off the flowers I forgot when I bolted."

"Semantics. If you want to prove it, then go on a second date with him, or a third if you want to count the ball he ended up bringing you to. I mean, I know it was *just* a visit to daddy, who was conveniently throwing a party, but you still spent the day with him. It looks as if you are pretty darn close to each other judging by these pictures."

Zadie chuckles. "Not that close. The photographers just picked the right angles, but it was nice spending time with him. I actually enjoyed myself."

"There you go. Go back to the computer, open up the site and message him. Set up a second date, or I will do it."

"Fine, but not right now. I have things to do, like deliver the potions I made yesterday to the post office so we can continue to have a roof over our heads. I also want to look at perhaps a windowsill pot since I have a feeling those nightshades are going to outgrow the little one I have them in. We need groceries if you actually want to eat, unless of course you are going to hunt for the pair of us."

"Not happening, Zadie. Lazy here, remember. I am just here as support!"

"Right. Support." She rolls her eyes, running her fingers through his fur. "I will message him once I have everything done. I get the impression Zevran will want to book it sooner rather than later."

"He's a prince. It's expected."

"Well, he's going to have to wait. Now, I suppose I should get ready. The news has delayed me enough." Zadie heads to the bedroom and dresses, grabbing her purse, and stuffing her phone into it. Padding back across the living room, she slips her shoes on, grabs her keys and heads to the car, driving into town with a list at her side.

Chapter Eleven

Charred Bones

Hours later, Zadie returns from the grocery store, dropping her bags on the kitchen counter. She smiles at the soft hisses of the nightshade and leans in. "I got you two presents, my little Beastlies. A window pot and one I need to make. First, I have to put the food away, then I can get you transferred. Afterwards, I can make your treats." Reaching out, she pets their leaves and hears their grumbles of discontentment, drawing a laugh from her lips. "Alright. Let me unpack and I will get started."

Once she has all the food put away, she returns to her car. There, she collects the pot and bag of dirt, carrying them back to the kitchen. Placing the dirt in the planter, she carefully transfers all the nightshades, separating them so they are side by side. Lifting the pot carefully, she sets it on her windowsill, smiling at the rustle of leaves as they spread out. "Much better. This planter is long enough so that you each have direct access to the sun."

She cleans up the dirt and carries the bag and the empty pot out back, setting it with the others. Returning to the kitchen, she pulls out the pre-cooked chicken and sets about pulling the meat from the bones, dropping it in a container for chicken caesar later. Picking up the bones, she waves them at the plants. "I am taking these out back to char them. I don't know how long it will take, so try to behave." She watches the plants quiver, their leaves rustling at the thought of a treat.

"Who knew plants were impatient?" She pushes the back door open and heads out to her small camping pit. Pulling the metal rack out, she gently lays the bones on it. Once that's done, she moves to the woodpile and collects a few pieces, setting them in the pit, low enough for her tripod grill to fit over it. Happy with the wood, she flicks her wrist and starts the fire, watching the flames lick skyward. Lifting the grill, she settles the three legs around the pit and lowers the chain so that the bones are just above the fire. Uncertain what the charred bones of Hell are like, she wants them to hold their shape and have the smoky burnt essence she suspects the plants crave.

Happy with her setup, she moves around her garden, watering her plants and checking on them all, inspecting their roots and leaves, keeping them free from any pests that might threaten them. As the scent of bones charring fills the air, she turns and makes her way back to the fire. Grabbing some tongs, she rolls the bones over and settles down on a chair, watching the flames flicker and dance, licking the edges of the grill.

"Why are you grilling bones?"

She startles at the voice beside her, jumping up and swinging the tongs in that direction, feeling her hand stop as he grabs them. "Mordek?"

"Impressive. Most can't tell us apart."

Zadie rolls her eyes and pulls the tongs back from his grasp. "It's not that hard."

"Really?"

"Yes, really."

"What are the tells?"

"Do you want the subtle or obvious ones?"

"Both. I'm intrigued."

Zadie turns back to her fire, rolling her bones over once more. "Right, you all stand the same height, but your postures are different. Compared to the other two, who are much stiffer, more soldier-like, your shoulders are more relaxed. Not that I am saying you're not a warrior, because your stance betrays that; you are just more casual. I guess that's why he sent you to spy on me."

"I am not spying. I am guarding."

"Guarding implies I know you are here. Considering you didn't announce your presence, it's spying."

"What else?"

"You have a scar on the eyebrow, Thane has one on his jawline, and Nicx has one below his lip, not quite on the chin. Your eyes have a faint silver fleck in the iris, Thane's are darker, almost obsidian, and Nicx has a subtle golden glow to his."

"Damn, that's impressive."

"It's called paying attention. There are other differences, but those are the main ones."

"Now you have me curious. Tell me more."

"Scent. Each of you is different, varying in degrees of smoke, sulphur and brimstone. Also, Nicx clenches his jaw when he scans around, like nerves are playing into it. Almost as if he's not fully comfortable being a prince's guard. The tone and pitch of voices, Thane has the book boyfriend voice. You two do not."

Mordek arches a brow. "Book boyfriend voice? What is that?"

Laughing, she shakes her head. "I guess there are no audiobooks in Hell."

"Nope."

"Alright, he's got a voice that could lure a girl to her doom. Sexy, deep, raspy, with just a hint of a growl. Much like Zevran's. Granted, Zevran's is better, but that could be because I am attracted to him and not Thane."

"Are you saying my voice is not sexy?"

"That's exactly what I am saying. Yours has the playful banter of brotherly love. Or best friend written all over it."

"Ouch, a stab to my heart."

"Exactly my point. You tease and jest, but you know Zevran is my mate, so you treat me as a sister instead."

"I can't believe you got all that from our meeting."

"You learn to catch minor details when you are a witch because if you don't, it can be costly." She shrugs her shoulders, turning the bones over again. "Some love us, some hate us, some hunt us."

"I suppose. So what are you cooking? Something for a spell or potion?"

"Bones for the nightshades."

"Wait, you're feeding them?"

"Of course. I am not letting them die."

"Do you know what the bones do to them?"

"Nope. I just know Zevran said, charred bones. So that's what I am doing."

"Does he know?"

"Why would he know?"

"I will return."

"Of course you will." She watches him fade and turns her attention back to the bones. Seeing them evenly blackened, she uses her tongs and lifts them carefully off the grill, placing them in the bowl. Once all the bones are safe, she draws on her magic and snuffs out the fires. Carrying the bones back into the kitchen, she can hear the plants hissing excitedly. "Not done yet, Beastlies. First, I have to crush them. That's what Zevran said."

She sets the bowl down near them, watching as they lean over, their leaves rustling, with soft hints of screams escaping them. Pulling her mortar and pestle out of the cupboard, she places them next to the bowl. Testing their temp, she lifts a few and drops them in, humming softly as her hand twists the pestle around, grinding down on the bones.

Hearing a knock on her door, Zadie rests her pestle in the bowl and brushes her hands off on a tea-towel. "I will be right back." She chuckles at their discontent. "I can't help it. Blame whoever is at the door." Leaving them to their rustling leaves and hissing, she pads to the front door. Opening it, she gasps in surprise at Zevran standing there, dressed in black leather pants, combat boots and a royal blue silk shirt, again, with the top three buttons undone. Damn those buttons. She wants to do them up, so that she doesn't have to resist the temptation of touching him. Getting over her shock, she asks him. "What are you doing here?"

"I came to check on you after yesterday."

Zadie narrows her eyes, immediately noticing the slight shift in his posture as he avoids direct eye contact. "Bullshit. That might be part of it, but not all of it."

"I heard you were feeding the nightshades."

"Yes, it's what you do when you have plants or animals. You feed and water them."

"Bones?"

Her gaze shifts past him, seeking the tattletaling red eyes. Finding them off to the left behind Zevran, she lifts her hand and sends a blast of fire his way, knowing he's probably immune to fire but perhaps it's enough of a warning to keep his mouth shut in the future. She smiles at the yelp of shock and the eyes fading away, knowing he's still close enough to guard the prince. "Well, I am only going by what you said. Crushed charred bones. Your exact words when I asked what you feed them. Now, if you don't mind, Nightshades have no patience, and I left the bowl in the kitchen with them."

"May I join you?"

"If you insist." Zadie spins and walks away from the door, leaving it up to him whether he accepts. Back at the counter, she smiles at the nightshades. "Alright, Beastlies. It's just Zevran. I'll get this done for you soon." She lifts her gaze as he walks into the kitchen, noticing him stop and stare at the pile of bones next to her. Huffing softly, she picks up a few and grinds more into her bowl.

Zevran leans in, frowning. "Where did you even get those?"

She gives him a look. "The grocery store. It's pre-cooked barbecue chicken."

His brow arches, a dangerous gleam flickering in his cobalt-red eyes. "You are feeding the Hell-born nightshades... grocery chicken bones?"

"What? You thought I just had a stash of charred femurs lying around? Despite being a witch, that's not something I stock on hand, so I am testing the waters with them. Don't judge me. Besides, it was this or wait until your father throws another ball and I sneak off with a rib cage. Since I don't know or trust your *guardian* nightshades to steal from them, this is the next best thing."

"Wait, are you saying you trust..." He gestures to the plants in the window. "These?"

"Yes, I do."

For a moment, silence stretched between them. Then Zevran pinches the bridge of his nose and mutters, "The heir of Hell's plants are being raised on rotisserie scraps."

"Don't be so dramatic. They have not objected to anything I have given them. In fact, they loved the sweet milk. You should've seen them wiggle."

His mouth twitched, betraying the faintest curve of a smile. "Milk? Wiggle?"

"Happy plants wiggle," she says firmly. "You'll just have to trust me on that." She reaches out to pet a few of them lightly, earning a gentle rustling and soft hisses as they nuzzle her hand.

Zevran reaches out to stop her from touching them, knowing exactly how temperamental the plants can be. He growls and arches a brow, utterly unamused when the plants wrap their vines around her wrist. "Really?"

"Hey little Beastlies. It's alright. He just doesn't know you like I do." Zadie slides a narrowed gaze his way. "Don't be so jealous. You gave them to me. What did you expect?"

Zevran stands there with the demon equivalent of a jealous cat glare. "They're weeds with attitude, Zadie, not pets. You don't need to coo over a pot of hissy, thorny nightshades."

The nightshades hiss at him in perfect unison, while she just laughs and pets them. "Jealous much?"

"Not at all."

"You're sounding it." Removing her hand from their vines, she finishes the rest of the bones. Moving to the drawer, she digs for a spoon, and stirs her mixture.

Zevran places a hand on hers to stop her from feeding them, earning a round of screams from the plants, and a shattering of glass from somewhere in the back of the house. "You know that adding charred bone makes them rage. It's why the gardener requests we feed them that. To help protect the castle with angry plants that will consume anything that gets near them."

Zadie yanks her hand back, the bones drifting from the spoon onto the edge of her bowl, with some spilling onto the counter. "Great. Look what you made me do. They will not bite me. Just let me do my thing." She grabs a plate and sweeps the bone dust onto it, dumping it back in the bowl. Lifting her spoon again, she shifts some of the plant's leaves aside and tips the spoon, dropping it on the dirt. The closest plants hiss, their thorns protruding momentarily, before a quiet scream of delight fills the air.

Working her way along the pot, she makes sure each and every one of them gets a spoonful before stepping back. "See, wiggle! And they didn't bite me, Mr. Know-it-All!" She mutters, pouring the remaining bone dust into a resealable bag and carrying it over to the fridge to store. As she closes the door, a blur of black fur catches her eye, turning to see Soot jump on the counter beside the plants. "Soot! Do not pester them."

"I'm not! Just saying hello to your date."

"He's not my date today. He showed up because he's jealous of the plants."

"I am not. I was concerned when Mordek said you were charring bones for them." He eyes the plants humming quietly in the window, turning his attention to the cat staring at him with golden eyes.

"Right, Mr. Tattletale over there in the corner of my kitchen thinks he's safe because I can't see him hiding in the fern." Her eyes lock onto the red ones lurking. "He's just lucky I won't use that type of magic inside my house. I don't even know how he made it past my wards."

"You invited me, and I invited him."

"Well, uninvite him."

"I can't do that; I want you to stay safe."

"I can take care of myself."

"Alright then. Guest." Soot interrupts their bickering, his golden eyes studying Zevran carefully. "So when are you taking Zadie on a second date?"

"Soot!"

"It's not been discussed." Zevran slides a glance at Zadie.

"You should take her to the restaurant on the pier. I believe it's called The Coral Crown. She's always wanted to go but never has. Also, the haunted museum is perfect for her tastes."

"Good idea, I will make reservations. You clearly know her well, so what color should I wear?"

"Purple. Dress to kill!"

"I am standing right here." Zadie places her hands on her hips, glaring at the pair of them. "And DO NOT dress to kill. There have been enough deaths in my life, Soot! You know this! Besides, I haven't agreed to anything." She moves back to the counter and collects her mortar and pestle. Placing it in the sink, she sets about washing her dishes and placing them in the drying rack.

"Yes, you have. Earlier on the couch. You said you would message after your chores were done. It looks like they are." Soot answers.

"Who's side are you on, Soot?"

"Yours, Zadie, but Zevran here is your mate. You really need to get to know each other better."

"Fine. But not until the weekend. I have things to do." She pulls a tea towel off the stove and dries her hands.

"She doesn't. She just doesn't want to admit she likes you."

"Soot! Sides. MINE! Not his!" Zadie exclaims, glaring at her cat.

Zevran chuckles, turning his attention from the cat to Zadie, the blue in her eyes flashing like ice against fire, standing in casual cotton pants and a black t-shirt with the image of a teal dragon, hidden behind spider webs. "I understand. I will pick you up on Friday at four."

Her gaze snaps to him. "You don't even have reservations yet. Do you know how exclusive that place is?"

"Not at all, but it can't be that hard."

Rolling her eyes, she hangs the towel back up and strides from the kitchen, shaking her head. She pauses and points to the fern. "You will NOT step foot in my bedroom or I will banish your ass back to Hell. That room is off limits to your spying. So is the bathroom, for that matter. Is that understood?" Waiting until she sees the eyes shift, like the head is nodding, she stomps out of the kitchen to her room, and slams the door.

Soot stands, arching his back as he stretches on the counter. "Well, that's it for her extroverted side. Introvertness just kicked in. See you Friday." He jumps off the counter and pads into the living room, eyeing the closed door.

Zevran turns to Mordek, watching him materialize before him, lowering his voice to keep Zadie and Soot out of their conversation. "Monitor her. Father is still looking, though I might have led him straight here when you came to get me."

"I will." He looks down at the char mark on his skin. "Your witch has power. She sent fire my way, but it actually burned. I don't think she realized or intended to hurt me, just a warning blast. Everyone knows we are immune to fire."

"What?"

"Yes, there is something else in her magic."

"Interesting. She has power; I have felt it."

"And witnessed it in the rings. I wonder if your father burned the same way."

"No. I got the impression she reflected his spell. The guards, yes, because she used ice. If Father finds out her fire hurts us, he will want her head. Keep this between us."

"I will. If anyone asks, it's ice damage."

"Thanks. Now, apparently, I need to plan a date for my feisty witch."

"She's a handful and perfect for you, Zev."

"She is. Hell, she even tamed the nightshades." He glances back toward the plants, humming and swaying in the window, their leaves rustling every few seconds.

"Never thought I would see that. I bet she could tame the castles' nightshades if she put her mind to it."

"Another thing we will keep from Daddy Dearest."

"Good plan."

Both of them fade from the kitchen, Zevran off to set things up for a date, and Mordek to watch over the house, settling in the living room with Soot.

Chapter Twelve

The Reluctant Yes

Days later, after getting a reservation for dinner on the patio and tickets to the museum, Zevran rifles through his closet and pulls things out, wanting to dress very specifically for the dinner. It needed to be special. He didn't want to repeat himself with Zadie. He'd worn the hoodie and jeans when he first met her, a casual disguise, letting her see the unvarnished edges of him. The second time, when he escorted her to meet his father, he chose black dress pants and a wine-red shirt, half-buttoned, the very picture of a rebellious prince.

But tonight? Tonight is different. Tonight he aims to win her over, and he's not intending to play fair. Mordek has peeked into her books, watched her on social media, noted the videos she navigates towards, and that style of dress now rests on his bed, waiting for him to don it.

Later, Zadie opens the door and finds him standing there as though he'd stepped straight from another world. The black suit jacket sits sleek over his frame, but it's what lies beneath that unravels her composure. The corset vest hugs him close, boned with violet accents that glow subtly against the black brocade. Each lace, each line, deliberate, structured, refined, and yet dangerously intimate. The rich purple in his shirt and tie, matching the shade of twilight caught between night and magic; a color that suits him, and her. Too perfect to be chance.

"Ready?" he asks, offering his hand as though he had all the time in the world to wait for her to recover, while skimming over her violet dress, fitted in the bodice with lacings and flaring over her hips to the ground. A wide black belt hugs her waist, matching her usual combat boots. A black choker with violet gems wraps around her throat, with a single chain dangling from it, ending in an amethyst wrapped in a heart.

Her eyes lock on the smile that curves across his lips at her reaction, knowing exactly what the corset is doing to her as heat pools in her core. She steps back, knowing it isn't just clothing; it's a statement: I am restraint. I am temptation. I am both at once, and you will be mine. "Fuck me."

"I'd like to Zadie, but not without your consent."

"Zevran…"

Soot strolls into the living room. "Hot damn! Would you look at the matching pair? He even looks human today, what with hiding his horns. Enjoy your evening, Zee, but not too much. We wouldn't want the world to end."

"Soot!" Zadie huffs and grabs the keys from beside the door, stuffing them into a little black purse. She reaches for his hand, only to pull back, shaking her head. "No, I lost about a third of my potions when you went to stop me from feeding my nightshades. I had to order new jars."

"Fair enough. No touching in the mortal realm." He turns to the sleek black sports car in the driveway. "Your chariot awaits."

"You have a car?" Zadie snaps her gaze to his.

"Well, we can't exactly fade into the restaurant. Besides, we have an abode in the mortal realm. I just pulled a car from there."

"I guess I am a little surprised you can drive."

"Zadie, my love. We are not that far behind the times in Hell." He moves over to the passenger door and opens it, stepping back to allow her inside. Once she's secure, he closes it and moves around to the driver's side, hopping in. "Are you ready for a night on the town? Fine dining, then the haunted museum."

"You actually got reservations?"

"I did. Are you impressed?" He turns, his copper eyes locking on hers, waiting for her response.

She blushes, breaking eye contact and fanning her flushed skin with her clutch. "Yes… is it hot in here?"

"Indeed, it is." Starting the car, he presses a button on the dash. With a soft whir, the roof unlocks, folds back on itself, and tucks neatly into the rear pod. "Better?"

"Much. Thank you."

Chuckling, Zevran backs the car up and turns it around, heading down the road at a comfortable pace. He glances over at Zadie, twisting the straps of her purse around her fingers, weaving them through figure eights before undoing them again. He spots the slight tap of her toe, and the way she keeps her face just slightly away from him, with the occasional blush crossing her cheek, finding himself curious about what's causing it. "Penny for your thoughts?"

Zadie snaps her eyes over to him. "Really?"

"Yes. You are clearly nervous tonight, when you weren't last time."

"What's going to happen between us, Zevran?"

"Well. We are going to eat, then see some strange things from what I gather."

"No, I mean, if this works out. Clearly, your father hates me. He tried to blow me up with a fireball. Am I always going to worry about him trying to kill me?"

"Let me deal with my father. If he wants to press the issue, I will leave Hell and live up here."

"I thought you were just saying that as a threat."

Zevran slows the car and pulls over on the side of the road. Putting it in park, he turns to face her. "Zadie. You are my mate. I would do anything for you."

"What about the fact that you are a demon with a much longer lifespan? I am just a human."

"First, you are *not* just a human. You are my mate. Second, when a mate bonds, their lifespans adjust. I will lose some of mine, and you will gain years to yours. We will live together for however long we live."

"I didn't know that."

"Few do. It's a closely guarded secret."

"Just like nightshades in my kitchen."

A smirk crosses his lips. "Yes. Just like them. Any more questions?"

Zadie shakes her head. "Nope."

"Good, now let's go get ourselves some dinner. I hear the food is to di... vine at this place."

Zadie giggles, "Good catch. Thanks for settling my nerves."

"You're welcome. Honestly. Don't think about it. We will just go with the flow, and whatever happens, happens."

"Deal."

Zevran shifts the car into gear and glances back. Seeing the road clear, he pulls back out and drives them to the restaurant. After parking the car, he looks up at the restaurant, its log house style matching the pier it sits on. "Interesting aesthetic. Wait here; I will get the door." He hops out and moves around, opening the door for her and assisting her out of the car.

At the sound of trees cracking nearby, Zadie yanks her hand back. "Sorry, I don't want the pier to break."

Zevran laughs. "Wouldn't that be a sight? The pier snapping and the restaurant and all its guests, tumbling into the ocean. I guess that would be one way to negate the reservations I had to work for."

Zadie smiles, a teasing glint in her eyes. "Oh, the Prince had to work for something. I bet that's unusual."

Zevran grasps his chest, flashing a mock-pained expression her way. "You wound me, mate. I have to work to win you over. That's two things."

Zadie fights the twitch in her lips, resisting the laughter bubbling inside. "Wow. So, I am work now? And what makes you so sure you have?"

"Of course you are." He leans in close, his breath blowing on her eyes. "If I haven't, then I bet if I keep wearing corsets, I might just win your heart faster than your mind. It seems you have a thing for them."

A blush crosses her cheeks, her hand lifting to fan her face. "Damn, you fight dirty."

"Anyway I can, my darling mate."

"Clearly. Though is it really you if it's actually Mordek spying on me and reporting back? I thought I felt him watching over my shoulder a few times."

Zevran gestures to the stairs and they walk up them to the restaurant's doors. "It's all part of fighting dirty. Gain knowledge where you can and use it to your advantage. Besides, very few places make men's corsets. I had to actually hunt them down."

"No, but the one that does, makes some pretty amazing ones. And the fellow modeling them is pretty damn hot."

"I know. Mordek gave me the name. They even make purple, as you can see." He smiles, adjusting his jacket back over his shoulders, as though daring anyone to question the choice.

Zadie rolls her eyes at his motions, knowing what he is seeking. For those who understand the language of clothing, the message is clear: he is no pawn at the table. He is the game itself and a damn fine game. One that caught her off guard when she opened the door. But now that she has the chance, she studies his apparel. "Alright, you might have a better body than the one they have modeling. I won't know until you sit on a stool and spin slowly."

"I can do that for you."

"Of course you can," Zadie mumbles under her breath as he opens the door for her. She steps in and turns, waiting as he steps in close behind her, the scent of brimstone, mixed with a hint of toasted marshmallows, enveloping her. She closes her eyes and reaches out for the nearby wall, steadying herself, as his breath at her neck weakens her knees.

"I would do anything for you, Zadie." Zevran straightens as the hostess appears, immediately noticing her giving them both a once-over but lingering on him.

"Can I help you?" She asks, her tongue flicking over her lips as her eyes darken on Zevran.

"Yes, I have a reservation for my fiancée and me, under Zevran." Scenting the desire in the air, he steps closer to Zadie, clearly implying they are together.

"Fiancée?" Her eyes flick down to Zadie's hand.

Zevran narrows his eyes at her reaction. "The ring is getting sized. Apparently, I misjudged her size."

"Oh..." She moves behind the desk and scans over the tables, finding his name listed. "Ah yes. Out on the patio, facing the cove where the otters frolic." She collects menus and gives them a nod. "Right this way."

Zevran guides Zadie in front, placing her between himself and the hostess. At the table, he steps aside, letting her choose her seat. When she does, he pulls the chair out and gestures for her to sit, sliding it in as she settles. Only then does he take his place across from her, smiling at the wonder on her face as she takes in the view. "Like it?"

Zadie drags her eyes away, and over to Zevran's. "It's beautiful."

The hostess steps up, sidling in close to Zevran. "Can I get you some drinks to start?"

"Yes, please. Can I get a *Stay In Your Lane Sangria*?" Zadie lifts her chin at the woman's nerve, her eyes locking onto Zevran's as she places the order.

The hostess blinks, her smile faltering for a split second before she smooths it back in place. "Of course... And for you, sir?"

Without missing a beat, Zevran smirks, his voice low and steady, daring the hostess to miss his meaning. "And I'll have a *Happily Claimed Highball*." He leans back in his chair, watching her fumble with her pen and paper before scurrying away.

Zadie can't help the laugh that bubbles out. "So, my darling fiancé. What does my ring look like?"

"Stunning. Big purple diamond surrounded by smaller white ones."

"And did I gush over it?"

"Oh, you did. You jumped into my arms and kissed me many times."

"Good to know."

"Are all humans like that?"

"You have no idea, do you?"

"Of what?"

"Just how attractive you are. And dressed like that. Damn, you look like you walked right out of a dark romance book. Mafia lord, billionaire, the bad guy that all of us romance readers want. She can't help herself."

"So, I should stick to a hoodie and jeans when out with you?"

"I don't think that's going to matter. Even the ladies in the coffee shop turned their gazes to you when you walked in."

"Really?"

"Yes, really. Oh, the Prince's trials of having women fawn all over him in the mortal realm."

"Except the one I want."

Zadie sighs and leans forward, placing her hands on the table and fiddling with the napkin there. "I want to, but it scares me, Zevran. You need to understand it's unfamiliar territory for me. If you were a mortal, your death would be imminent."

Zevran leans in, his eyes staring into hers. "I am aware. That is why I will take the time to do this right."

"Thank you."

Dinner arrives, and the pair savor their time together. Every movement is elegant, every glance laced with quiet possession as they sip from crystal glasses, candlelight glinting over artfully plated food. Beyond the railings, otters chatter and frolic in the nearby cove. When the meal ends, Zevran rises with her, guiding her from the restaurant as heads turn toward the aura that seems to radiate from them both.

Chapter Thirteen

The Wraithmore Estate

Back in the car, Zevran drives them away from the pier, taking them into the heart of the city and out the other side to a restored mansion just as the moon rises in the sky. Out front is a sign, held up by twisted iron and dressed in black with chipped gold writing announcing the place.

The Wraithmore Estate.
Museum of the Macabre & Haunted History

"Is it open?"

"Yes, their hours are until one, just past the witching hour, to experience all the hauntings it offers."

"And what exactly do they offer?"

"Let's see. What did I read on their webpage?" He winks at her as his finger taps his chin. "A haunted museum with its halls draped in shadows and whispers, where cursed artifacts glimmer in their cases and ghost stories linger in the air."

"That is *not* what it said."

"No, not really. The site said they offer a display of cursed artifacts, host ghost stories on the hour and have a haunted escape room. Sounds intriguing."

"That sounds fun!"

"What, you like that better? Do you know how long it took me to write that sentence and then memorize it?"

"All of five minutes?"

"Indeed, but it sounds good. I should be their PR person." Zevran chuckles and hops out of the car, striding around to open her door. "I am intrigued by these so-called cursed artifacts."

"Yes, so am I. It's one place I mentioned to Soot that I wanted to see, but I never have."

"Well then. Shall we?"

"We shall."

Zadie and Zevran enter a small lobby, where a receptionist, dressed in ghostly attire, sits behind the desk, typing on the computer. Her eyes flick their way, drawing a smile to her lips. "Welcome to Wraithmore. Do you have passes, or did you need to buy them?"

Zevran pulls out a pair and places them on the counter. "I bought them a few nights ago."

She picks up the tickets, eyes skimming over them before tearing one corner to split the barcode in half. Handing them back, she slides a pamphlet from the counter and passes one to each of them.

"That's the schedule and a map of the museum. All rooms are open access, but if you check the second floor, for example, that's the story room. Although slamming a door might spook the listeners, it disrupts the storyteller, so we ask that you slip in quietly. The escape room is on the third floor, and the wraith there will take your name and assign you a time slot, so be sure you're back by then. Artifacts are scattered throughout the rooms, their histories written nearby. Please don't touch them. Many are rumored to still carry curses, and no one has figured out how to lift them."

"Wait, they are open access?" Zadie asks.

She smiles Zadie's way. "No, they are cordoned off, or glassed in, but that doesn't stop the zealots from trying. If someone does, an alarm goes off and the doors lock on the room." She points to the ceiling and the small black dome. "There are also cameras in each room that I have access to here on this computer."

"Why the cameras?" Zevran follows her gesture to the shiny dome he didn't notice when he walked in.

"To monitor the place. Some try to touch things, especially the dress. Others get lost, and panic, and we need to send people to help them. It is a haunted mansion after all."

"I can't wait. I hope we see the ghosts you have pictures of on your website."

"They come out between 11 and 1 pm. Usually on the second floor, which is why the stories are there. It's always a delight to hear a room full of people screaming when a real ghost steps through the wall. Many believe it's a projector, like the ones we have in the windows, but if it's not in a window, it's not us."

"Good to know."

"Have fun, you two. Just enter through the side door there when you are ready."

Zevran leans in and murmurs. "Tell me, little witch... is it the living you fear, or the dead?"

Zadie chuckles and whispers back. "Perhaps it's demons. But this is going to be fun. Let's do it."

"Ouch, my poor fragile heart." Zevran leads her over to the doors and pushes them open, stepping into the darkened interior after her.

"Somehow, I doubt your heart is fragile." She teases him.

As the lighted lobby fades, they take a moment to adjust to the dimness surrounding them. Lanterns and old sconces cast golden shadows across polished stone floors. It smells faintly of incense and aged paper. The halls are wide but hushed, every sound amplified: heels on marble, the rustle of clothing, a breath caught when a shadow shifts. Some rooms hum faintly with residual energy; others are colder than they should be, as though the walls themselves remember.

Zadie moves down the hall, stopping at the portraits that hang there, watching a few of their eyes moving to follow as they step to the next one, each with a nameplate and how they are tied to the mansion. She stops at one similar to hers with ash-white hair, reading the plaque on the bottom.

The White Haired Witch

Little is known of the woman who once walked these halls, with her hair pale as moonlight and her gaze said to pierce straight through the soul. Legends disagree on her intent. Some claim she healed the sick, whispering blessings over infants' cradles. Others insist she bargained with shadows, cursing those who crossed her.

When this mansion was restored, her likeness appeared unbidden in stories, diaries, and even sketches found hidden in the walls as if she had never truly left. Whether guardian or tormentor, she remains a presence here, her spirit woven into the fabric of the house.

Step softly. Decide for yourself if her legacy is one of mercy... or malice.

Zevran leans in, studying her features. "The two of you look as if you could be related."

"Right, because she has white hair."

"No, seriously. Her eyes are the same color and shape. Her nose and lips are different, but her jawline matches yours. I bet she's an ancestor."

"Except we didn't live here. My parents grew up on the other side of the country. I moved here after Desmond blew up to get away from the media. Though now I am back in it, thanks to you."

"You never know. There is no date on this plaque. Could be before your grandparents, or even their grandparents." Zevran draws his eyes from the painting, absolutely certain she's an ancestor. "You're talking about the demon rags. Pay no attention to them. They will move on quickly enough."

"Yes. I am. Somehow I have my doubts about that. You are a prince. I am just a human witch. It's a PR feast."

"We have been through this. Human yes, but not just a witch. If you were, your fire would not have harmed Mordek."

"What?" Zadie gasps and glances around for the red eyes that she knows are lurking. "I thought you were immune to fire."

"We are. Just not yours, apparently."

"I'm sorry. I didn't mean to hurt him. I didn't think..."

"Shh Zadie. We both know that. If you had, you would have used ice, but we are curious why your fire hurts."

Her shoulders slump, her eyes darting back to the portrait of the witch, glancing around the hallway, seeing another couple stepping out of the room. "I might know why, but not here. Back at the cottage."

"Deal."

They wander down to the room the other couple stepped out of, and step inside, seeing a group of people standing along the far wall, reading a few posters.

In the center of the room, set on a wooden pedestal with a black rope strung between stanchions, sits an ornate iron mask. Both of them approach the plaque, reading the simple tag on it.

The Mask of the Hollow King
An iron mask once worn by a monarch who was rumored to have bargained his soul away. If you stare into its hollow eye sockets too long, you feel watched.

Zevran leans in and whispers in Zadie's ear. "This one is correct. He bartered his soul with Daddy Dearest, so I doubt his soul is watching, since he's currently in Hell. If you want to meet him, I can take you there."

Zadie tilts her head, feeling the closeness of Zevran, the painting on the wall shifting slightly, earning a few screams from the group. She replies softly. "Well, I don't feel any magic in this room. Not like the hallway."

Zevran watches the group race from the room. "No magic but ours."

"True." Zadie laughs and steps away, wandering over to read the history of the owner of the mask.

"Why are you reading that? I can just get him to answer the questions you have."

"To compare accuracy. Besides, it's interesting. Might as well explore everything."

Once she is happy, they walk out of the room, moving to the next one, following a family into it. Inside, the room's walls are covered in mirrors, each reflecting different aspects, much like a funhouse. Zadie laughs as her reflection changes shape until she gets to the one in the middle. Larger than the rest, with a blackened silver frame rather than wood or iron like the others. A small plaque beneath it says.

The Mirror of St. Corvus.
Rumor has it that if you linger too long in front of it, it will trap your reflection within.

Zadie shakes her head, meeting her reflection in the mirror, lifting her gaze to Zevran's, once again drawn to his attire and the fact that he looks perfect. "Well, if I were that mirror, I would trap yours in it with me."

"You don't need to, Zadie. You already have me. Do you think it would steal your curse instead?"

"Ooh, good thought!" She moves over to the book nearby, seeing a list of viewers' testimonials, each swearing the reflection moved differently than them, some even saying it waved or winked. "Damn, I want it to wave at me."

"Do you feel magic here?"

Zadie snaps her gaze to the family, laughing at their reflections, making funny faces in the mirror. "Yes. There is definitely an aura surrounding the mirror."

"I can feel it too. Shall we move on to the next one?"

Zadie looks at the pamphlet in her hand. "Looks like the next room is a witch's wedding dress. I wonder what that means exactly."

"I guess we are going to find out." He guides her out and down the hall, following the legend on the paper to the room indicated. Inside, a mannequin adorned a perfectly preserved wedding dress, despite the centuries that had passed. Instead of white, as modern dresses are, this one is a pale cream, its silk bodice looking as if it's freshly woven. Long lace sleeves cling to the mannequin's arms, embroidered with twisting roses and thorns so fine they look real. The skirt spills outward in layers that shimmer faintly, untouched by dust, the veil trailing behind in ghostly perfection. A string of pearls circles the neckline, though the one near the heart has blackened, standing out like a warning. Stepping up, she reads the tag at the base.

The Witch's Wedding Dress
Legend says a bride cursed it to ensure no woman who wears it lives past her wedding night.

Zevran leans close and says, "It would look ravishing on you... shame about the odds."

"And the odds are good I will die. There is powerful magic in this dress. Both in that it's in perfect condition while not in a glass preservation case as it should be and I suspect a witch really did lace black magic into the embroidery. There is darkness surrounding it."

"Well then, we will just have to find you a non-cursed dress."

"Zevran! We haven't even discussed marriage, and you already made me a fiancée earlier. I do not aim to be a wife by the end of the evening, despite your attire making me want to."

"Fine. Not tonight then. Mark my words though, Zadie. I will do everything it takes to make you my bride, no matter how long it takes."

"Awww, how sweet." The voice comes from their left. A little girl with her wide brown eyes full of curiosity. Her blonde ponytail tied with a pink bow, her dress matches it perfectly and her sneakers are scuffed from play.

Zadie blushes at the thought of someone having overheard their conversation. "Hello little one."

"Hi! Why don't you want to marry him? He's the handsomest man I have ever seen."

"It's complicated."

"Can I marry him then? If you don't want to?"

Zevran chuckles and squats down to face the child. "Why, thank you. What is your name, sweetheart?"

"Monica."

"That's a beautiful name for a pretty lady. I am Zevran. This is Zadie."

"So, can I marry you?"

"How about I make you a deal?"

Zadie steps in. "Zevran, she is too young to know…"

Zevran winks at her, turning his attention back to Monica. "No, you can't marry me, because I intend to marry Zadie here. She's my soulmate. The one made for me. But I have younger brothers who are single. When you are old enough, I will happily introduce you. How does that sound?"

Monica looks up at him, her brown eyes widening. "Really? Are they as handsome as you?"

"I believe so. Do you want to see a picture?"

She claps her hands together. "Yes, please."

Zevran slips a phone out of his suit jacket and clicks it on. Moving to the photos, he finds a picture of three of his brothers. "This is Talaris, Kharan and Rurik."

"Wow, they are as handsome as you. I like your clothes better, though."

"Well, that's because this is a casual photo. When I first met Zadie, I was in a hoodie and jeans. But now I am trying to impress her. They would dress up to impress you as well."

"Why are all your names so strange?"

"Well, my father has a thing about being different." Zevran replies.

Monica ponders his words as she stares at the picture. "I understand. I am the only Monica at my school. I just started, but there are three Tracys. I like the middle one the best."

"That's Kharan."

"Monica! What are you doing?" A voice from the small crowd to their left filters out, and a woman weaves through them in their direction. "I'm sorry if she's bothering you. She's just so curious."

Zadie smiles, trying to soothe the woman. "It's alright. She's adorable."

"Mama, I am going to marry one of Zevran's brothers. They are so handsome."

"You're going to do what?"

"Well. I wanted to marry Zevran, but he's going to marry Zadie. He said that when I am older, he will introduce me to Kharan. He's the handsomest of the three. I will be older tomorrow, right?"

"Monica, sweetheart, you don't go asking people to marry them."

"Why not?"

"Cause you are six. You can't get married until you are eighteen. Then you can ask," her mom replies.

"Oh..." She glances back towards Zevran and Zadie. "Well, when I am eighteen, I will marry Kharan."

Her mother looks Zevran's way, mouthing the word *'Sorry'* and takes her daughter's hand. "Come on, sweetie. Let's leave these two nice people and catch up with Auntie Athena."

Zevran tucks his phone in his pocket, watching as the woman scurries back to the group filtering out of the room. He turns to Zadie. "Well, you just about lost me to an adorable blonde-haired, brown-eyed child. Are you sure you won't marry me tonight?"

"Damn, I might need to. She was really cute." Zadie laughs, shaking her head, before growing thoughtful. "I certainly hope that wasn't a deal with a demon sort of thing, though."

"Nah, no handshake and no blood exchanged. In a few days, she will turn her sights to a new handsome guy. She is going to be a handful when she gets older."

"Yes, she is."

"Aright, enough wedding stuff. Let's hit the marionette room. I have an idea."

"Why do I not like that look of mischief in your eyes?"

He shrugs, tossing her a wink before guiding her away from the wedding dress and out of the room. They wander up to the second floor, past the storytelling room, until they reach a shadowed side wing at the end of the hall.

Inside, antique dolls and strange creatures suspended on invisible strings fill the space. Some are centuries old, with cracked porcelain faces staring blankly, while others look almost new. Their faded gowns and glassy eyes tagged with small plaques at their feet, marking their age.

Three groups of visitors drift among the displays, talking among themselves as they study the puppets. Zevran steers Zadie between them, stopping at one of the older-looking sets. As she leans closer, he lets his fingers brush her shoulder; subtle, deliberate, just enough to make her jolt, along with the others in the room, when the marionettes suddenly twitch to life.

"What are you doing?"

"Having fun."

Zadie's gaze darts to the people jumping back from the puppets, a slow smile crossing her lips at the realization. "You are evil."

"I am."

"We will need to be careful."

"We will."

She nods and steps back to the puppets, looking over the elaborate dragon before her, the gemstone eyes that gleam under the torchlight in the room, wondering if they are real. Feeling Zevran step in close, she watches the dragon dance before her, hearing a few screams in the room, followed by the pounding of feet fleeing. Biting her lips, she refrains from laughing at their behavior, instead muttering. "Okay, I might be just as evil."

Zevran laughs. "That's why you are perfect for me."

They stay in the room longer than any of the others, enjoying tormenting everyone that comes through, before heading out to the next item on display, each chuckling softly.

Pulling out her paper, she looks it over. "Looks like there are two more objects. The Book of Ash and the Siren's Bones. Which one do you want to see first?"

Zevran leans over her shoulder, reading the description of both. "Let's do bones, then end with the book. That should put us in time to catch a story or two. Did you want to do the escape room?"

"Let's wait and see what time it is. I have heard some of those can take hours, and I want to inspect some of the portraits and see the ghosts."

"Got it."

They walk down another hall, and round the corner, with two doors opposite each other.

Stepping towards the left, Zadie steps inside, her gaze landing on a skeletal ribcage, displayed like art, the bones faintly glimmering with salt.

A large placard reads:

Do not touch. Those who hear her song, drown in silence.

Zadie steps backwards suddenly, bumping into Zevran, her hands snapping to her ears, as the torches around them flicker and extinguish. She scoots past him, placing a wall between her and the bones, as others around them scream in the darkness.

Immediately after, a voice drifts around them. "Keep calm everyone, we appear to have a power failure. We are working to get the backup generators running. Do not move from where you are. Lights will be back shortly. Sorry, this is not actually on us, and yes, we have paid the utility bill."

Zevran approaches Zadie, reading the apparent fear in her, touching her cheek to draw her attention to him. "Zadie?"

She lifts her hands off her ears slightly, and tilts her head, before dropping them. "I am not going in there."

"You don't have to. Let's go see the book instead, though I suppose we should wait for the lights to return."

Zadie nods, sliding further away from the room. "We should, but I can see in the dark."

"Really?"

"Being a witch does have its perks."

"Can I ask what happened?"

Zadie glances around as they make their way to the next room. "The plaque speaks the truth. There is a song tied to those bones. The second I heard it, I knew. The song calls you to the sea, where the sirens will drag you to their depths and drown you. I felt the pull immediately, even just on a few notes. Thankfully, it's not loud, and the screaming people drowned it out."

"I didn't hear a song, which is surprising because sirens usually draw men to their doom."

"Sirens can be of any sex. I don't know why I heard it; I just did."

"Perhaps it's because I didn't step into the room like you did."

"Don't."

"I won't. I wonder if there is a way to disable the song, so it can't lure the unsuspecting to their doom."

"Strong magic might, but the song is supernatural. I suspect the average human will not hear it." She lifts her gaze to his, smiling at the concern in the copper depths of his. "Aww, is the demon concerned about mortals?"

Zevran chuckles, leaning in towards her. "Only one, but she is concerned about them, so that makes me too ."

"Good answer."

Chapter Fourteen

Prophetic Curses

They reach the room of the last exhibit and step inside, seeing two other groups there, huddling together in the darkness. In the center of the room is an oversized leather-bound book, sealed in a glass case, with what appears to be a page turner attached to it.

Even where she stands, Zadie can tell the pages are singed, and the lettering glows softly in the darkness. She turns, asking Zevran. "Can you see that?"

"Yes, I can."

Another voice pops up. "See what? Is there a ghost?"

"The glow on the pages of the book." Zadie replies.

"There's no glow. Stop trying to scare us."

She steps forward just as the lights flicker back on, illuminating the room with a soft glow. A plaque on the podium reads.

> *The Book of Ash.*
> *Said to have been written in fire and grief. The words shift endlessly, making the tome unreadable.*

She lifts her gaze to the book, watching the symbols and lines on the page shift and flicker like embers from a fire, before reforming into something legible. She skims through the words, trying to make sense of it until she sees her name written further down, alongside the words.

The Betrayers Fire.

"Damn."

Zevran steps up, recognizing the book and knowing only the cursed can read it. "What do you see, Zadie?"

"It's a li..." She stops as one group steps forward.

"Can you really read it? It's just squiggles and lines."

Zadie hesitates, knowing if she said what it really is, they would question it. Opting for the next best thing, she points to a few of the letters, hoping they show as glyphs to the group. "Its ancient glyphs. I took some classes at school. One means power. The other means war. Some just appear to be squiggles or lines, which I am sure has some meaning that I don't know. I think it might be tied to one of the wars in the past."

"Wow! I need to research the glyphs and come back."

"You should. They are quite interesting. And each pantheon has its own set. They seem to be a mix of them all. I guess that's why it's unreadable, because they all have their own meanings."

They giggle amongst themselves. "It's like mixing languages then?"

"Yes, pretty much."

"I wonder why they wrote it like that."

"I don't know. I guess that's why it's here in the haunted museum."

Once they leave, Zevran chuckles quietly, reading over the page. "So. It seems one of your ancestors broke a sacred pact with a love god or death deity and now your family line is being punished?"

"According to this book, yes. But I don't know. If that was the case, then how did my parents have me? We can't even get close without things happening."

"Skip a generation?"

"It's possible."

"Can you ask them?"

"No, I haven't seen them since I was twenty. They just disappeared. There is still a missing persons report out on them. Cold case now, I suppose, since there have been no leads in years."

"I'm sorry, Zadie. I didn't know."

"How could you? I haven't talked about my parents at all."

"Well, we can go to the oracles. They might help."

Zadie ponders it, her eyes staying on the words on the page before her. "Yes, I might just do that when I am ready. I am not at the point where I want to find out if they ran away and left me because of my curse, or if something actually happened to them."

"Fair enough. When you are ready, I will take you."

"Thank you."

"Now, on a lighter note, let's go listen to ghost stories."

"Lighter note, huh?" She laughs, giving a last glance towards the book, both neglecting to mention that Zevran's name was right beneath hers, with the words written:

The curse does not vanish, it transfers.

Heading back the way they came, they slip silently into the room and take a seat near the back, meeting the gaze of the storyteller, who nods in quiet acknowledgment. Tales of ghosts haunting this very mansion and witches whispering curses into village wells, spill from his lips. He continues without pause, his voice low and deliberate, threading words through the dimness. Each listener leans forward, caught in the spell of his cadence.

"...and it was here," he says, his tone dropping to a near-whisper, "in the upstairs hall, where the pale girl was last seen. She wore no shoes, made nary a sound as she passed. Some say she was searching for her lost locket; others, that she was warning of what was to come. But all who saw her agreed on this: when she turned her head... she had no face at all."

A ripple of unease shivers through the room. The dim lights flicker, though no wind stirs. Then, from the corner near the storyteller's chair, a figure coalesces; translucent, white-haired, her very presence chilling the air.

Gasps rise as the ghost silently regards the crowd. Her hollow eyes locking on Zadie, one hand lifting, a finger crooking to beckon her forward, before vanishing into the wall.

Those in the front row twist in their seats, following the ghost's gaze, and freeze when they see Zadie, her white hair seeming to float around her like a phantom's own. Screams erupt, chairs crash to the floor, and the audience scrambles to escape the pair.

"Well, damn," Zadie mutters under her breath.

The storyteller stands, lifting his hands to calm the chaos. "Easy, everyone. Easy! They walked in the door just like the rest of you. I'm sure it's just a coincidence the ghost looks like the young lady in the back."

Zadie crosses her arms, raising a brow at the storyteller. "A coincidence, huh? Sure. Let's go with that. As you can see, I'm very much real. More likely, it's the white witch in the portrait downstairs. Even my fiancée says she looks a lot like me." Her wry tone earns a few nervous laughs, breaking the tension without fully dispelling the unease.

The storyteller's smile wavers, his gaze lingering on Zadie before sweeping the room. "Perhaps it was the portrait. Or perhaps the house enjoys playing tricks on us... reminding us its stories aren't finished." He lets the silence stretch, the dim lights flickering once more before he clears his throat. "But that's enough for now. Shall we continue?"

"Yes, please."

The people right their chairs and settle in. Some of them give a wary look in Zadie's direction and step out of the room, opting to explore other rooms in the mansion. Once everyone settles, the storyteller leads into another story, captivating them all once more after a few sentences.

Several stories later, Zadie and Zevran slip out, wandering down the halls, and looking over the portraits. She stops at one that looks familiar, leaning in to read the name on the bottom and not recognizing it. As she does, a ghostly face appears in the picture, mirroring her own with its white hair and cobalt eyes. Her hand reaches up to caress Zadie, freezing her in place.

She leans out of the wall, whispering in Zadie's ear. "Mixed blood burns and boils. The moon shall bleed red, yet the world will not fall; it will turn. Love is no blade, but fear cuts deepest. The curse drinks not of death, but of the dread of losing. When fire takes form again, shadows shall walk beside the living, and the lost shall rise in hollow skin, seeking to take down that which took it down. One ancestor schemes, his plans woven deeper than the curse and barters with the grave. The root above yet poisons the branch below." With that, she pulls back into the portrait, disappearing from their sight.

Zadie stumbles back, her eyes glancing around the hallway, seeing Zevran staring intently at her. She rubs her arms and shivers. "I want to go home now."

"Zadie?"

"Please, Zev, let's leave."

He nods and guides her back towards the entrance. In the lobby, they bid the receptionist good night, and head to the car. Once inside, Zevran turns to her, reading the fear etched in her features. "What did she say? I could tell she was talking, but clearly her whispers were only for you, since it was silent in the hallway."

Zadie shakes her head. "It was a riddle. I need to write it down before I forget."

Zevran pulls his phone out and hands it over. "Use the notepad. Passcode is 26-666."

"Thanks. I left mine at home. It still seems odd that, you have a phone?"

"How do you think I joined the dating app?"

"Right, stupid me."

"Not stupid, Zadie. You are rather intelligent."

"And yet, I didn't clue in to the fact that you have a phone."

"It's a simple enough mistake, considering Hell isn't known for its electronics."

"True. But you joined an online dating app, so you have to have access somehow." She enters in the passcode, and types what she remembers as Zevran starts the car and drives her home. Silence reigns in the car as Zadie stares at the written words on Zevran's phone, a sinking feeling in her heart, knowing it's about their relationship. She lifts a hand to brush at the tear slipping out and turns the phone over, clutching it in her hands as she stares out the window into the darkness.

"Talk to me, Zadie."

"At home."

Zevran nods, turning his attention back to the road, sparing a glance as often as he can towards Zadie. Knowing whatever the white witch said spooked her, judging by the way she is curled up in the seat, staring out the passenger window. As he pulls onto her driveway, he winds his way through the woods, parking out front of her cottage. Getting out, he rounds the car and opens the door. "Let's get you inside."

She nods and stumbles to the door, fishing out her keys with her free hand. Fumbling them slightly, she slides them in the lock and opens the door, stepping into the sanctuary of her house. Moving to the couch, she slumps down onto it, turning Zevran's phone over in her hands, caressing it lightly.

Zevran follows and closes the door behind him. Following her, he sits down beside her and swivels to face her, resisting the urge to draw her into his arms. "Alright, what did she say?"

"I'm not sure exactly." She hands the phone over to him.

He reads the writing on his notepad several times. "This is what she said."

"As close as I can remember. I might have missed a word or two, but it's enough."

"You know what this means?"

"Some of it."

"Are you deliberately being vague?"

Zadie sighs and closes her eyes, resting her head on the back of the couch. "I need more time, but I can tell you this. Mixed blood is us. I have celestial blood in my bloodstream, and you are a demon."

"Damn. That explains why your fire hurt Mordek." Zevran replies.

Her eyes scan, spotting Mordek in the corner of the living room, hiding between the books on her bookshelf. "Sorry, I didn't think it would hurt you. I didn't know that side of me came out in my spells."

"All good, Zadie." Mordek replies as he appears before them.

"Right, back to this cryptic message."

"I am guessing the moon bleeding red is the blood moon, which is next week... Friday if I recall correctly. Something is happening to the world, but that could be anything. It could even be us, since it is before love is not a blade, and something about fear. I have a lot of fear because I don't want to hurt you with my curse. I mean, I might actually like you."

"No, it's not us." Zevran realizes Zadie's curse is ancient, powerful... and afraid of being broken. "It's the curse. It's living, and it doesn't want to be broken. I think it's scared that our mate-bond will win out."

"Okay, I can see that maybe. As long as I am single, it's pretty quiet. Even when I read books and dream about the characters, it doesn't react. But what about fire taking form?"

"Something to do with me. Demons and fire go hand in hand."

"Perhaps. What about the ancestors? I don't have any I know of."

"Oh, that would be Daddy Dearest. He's scheming to get me to marry a demon... although I will look into the lost shall rise and bartering with the grave. Dad is in charge of the souls in Hell. If there is something going on, I aim to find out what."

Zadie nods. "That leaves the roots above, poisoning the branch below."

"Are you sure it wasn't the roots below?"

"Positive. It struck me as odd because it's backwards."

"Alright. What if it's tied to your celestial heritage? You are above. I am below. The mortal realms in the middle."

"Yes, which means this relationship is cursed."

"It already is, but I am still willing to try."

"What if it means I can actually kill you, despite the loophole you seem to think is there?"

"Zadie, you won't. Of this, I am certain."

She rubs her temples, feeling a headache creeping in. "How... how can you be so certain?"

Chapter Fifteen

Blood Betrayal

Zevran reaches out, but pulls his hand back at the sound of nightshades suddenly screaming in the kitchen. He glances towards Mordek and rises, heading towards the window, narrowing his eyes on the Hellhounds rising from the ground outside. "Damn it."

Soot bolts into the living room. "Zadie, we are under attack!"

"What?" Zadie jumps up and moves towards the window beside Zevran, narrowing her eyes on the creatures outside, burning her grass down from the fire dancing around their feet. "Oh no, they don't." She spins and marches towards her door, hearing both Zevran and Mordek telling her to stop. She yanks the door open and sends a glare their way as they breathe flames over her property. "I am not letting Daddy burn my house down. He thinks I am human. His precious puppies are going back to Hell where they belong."

"I guess that means we are helping." Mordek says.

Zevran sighs. "I guess so."

Stepping outside, Zadie matches the glare of the dogs. "Alright, let's see what Daddy thinks of me. Come get me, you wretched beasts."

"Zadie, my love. You should not taunt them like that."

"Oh please. I read about the beasts of Hell. These here are your first line of defense. What you would call fodder." Zadie grins in delight, her eyes flicking momentarily over to the nightshades screaming on her windowsill. "I am sure my plants will love their charred bones!"

Seeing two launch at her, she draws on her magic, flicking her wrists as a rune flies through the air, slamming into the first one and freezing it in place. The second one follows through, but bounces off an invisible shield protecting Zadie, rolling away with a yelp.

Zevran growls and stalks forward, his horns reappearing as he extends his claws, his voice holding power as he commands the dogs to stand down. Not in the least surprised when they don't.

Mordek flicks over and reappears behind one stalking Zadie on her left side. He draws his blades and digs them into the hound's hide, causing it to spin and attack him.

Three more dogs launch at Zadie, and she smiles, waving her arm in an arc as a wall of fire appears between them, something she would not have normally used but since it burned Mordek, she is counting on the same from the hounds. Hearing their howls of pain, she laughs manically; her witchyness coming out to play. "Aww, poor little puppies, burned by fire. Let's see how you take this one." She rolls her hands around as if forming a ball, watching a small flicker of flames appear. She cups it and throws it at the cluster of three rolling around, trying to extinguish the flames on their coats, only to be engulfed once more.

Zevran jumps back at the fireball expanding, seeing nothing remaining of the dogs when the flames fade. "What the hell, Zadie?"

"I am an elemental witch, Zevran. I command all the elements." She cackles and lifts a hand, tapping two of her fingers together, while threading a small golden string through them. Thunder booms across the sky as she calls down a single bolt of lightning, watching it chain through the hounds, searing their forms as sparks dance over them.

Seeing them scatter, she lowers her hands to the ground. Murmuring a few words, walls of thorny vines rise, barring their escape path. "No running, my little pups. You pissed me off by showing up here, thinking you can take me out. Now you will pay."

Mordek drops the one he's attacking, seeing it fade upon its death, and stops. He watches in awe as Zadie easily commands the elements. When the walls surround them, he gives her a wink. "Nice one, Lass."

Her eyes darted his way, seeing the first dog launch at her again, only to have Zevran's claws yank it out of the sky, ripping into it beside her. "Thanks." Scanning the battlefield, she notes at least seven more and laughs. "Really. Only twelve? Is that what your dad thinks I am worth?"

"Zadie, you really don't want to push my father. He's the king of Hell for a reason."

"Yes. Well. I am Zadie! Witch Extraordinaire. Mate to his son, and he is going to have to accept that!"

"He will, Zadie."

"You really should just return to Hell before I return you the painful way." Her gaze lands on a group of four trying to flank her. Lifting her hand, she points one finger up and twirls it, creating a small tornado of air, snapping her fingers as sparks jump from her to the tornado. She cuts her hand down through the center, splitting it into two, and sends them out to her flanks, watching it grow in size and capture the hounds. She blows on her hands, fanning the flames. "Burn, puppies, burn." A whirlwind of cinders and screaming wind tears around the hounds, reducing them to blackened ash, which scatters and then vanishes in a hiss of sulfur smoke. "And then there were three."

Mordek lifts his gaze from the one dying at his feet, his blade plunging into its heart. "Two. This one's dead."

"One, and it looks like he's running." Zevran shreds the one next to him, his body fading, along with the remaining one, who sinks back into the earth.

Zadie turns to the one encased in ice, feeling the panic as she steps closer. Her fingers trace over the ice, melting only that around its head, wanting to ensure he can hear her. "You can tell Daddy his toys break too easily and that if he wants me on a leash, he'll need more than puppies. Better yet, he should come himself. I bite harder than his pets."

"Zadie..." he exhales, half exasperation, half awe. "Again, you really shouldn't taunt my father."

"This is MY ground, Zevran. He needs to know that if his minions step in it, they will die. Himself included."

Zevran sighs and steps up to her. "I realize that, but these..." He gestures to the hound beside them, "make better kindling than killers. As you found out. He will send stronger and stronger warriors after you each time you send them back until one defeats you."

"He can try. I will be strengthening my wards and expanding them to include my property. They won't get in."

"Good. I will talk to him again as well."

Zadie rolls her eyes. "Right. He seems like the type to listen to reason. Maybe I should just do what the paparazzi of Hell whisper about. Walk through the front doors and claim the throne. White hair would really brighten up the place."

"Thrones aren't chairs, Zadie. They're cages with better upholstery."

"Well, if Daddy wants me gone, he should guard his throne better. One day, I won't just fight his hounds. I'll be sitting in his seat, and he'll be the one on the leash."

"Don't joke about that. He'd kill half his kingdom just to keep you from it. Remember, my father doesn't play fair, so please think about that before you go knocking on his door without me at your side."

Zadie smiles his way. "You don't think I don't know that, Zevran. Hell doesn't bend to anyone. It breaks them. I have no intention of taking over the throne, but if he attacks me again, he will find out just how resilient and strong humans can be."

"Damn, I could hug you right now."

She lifts her hand, stepping away. "No. Touching is off limits in my house, or outside it. I already had to replace a few orders and replant some trees last time. Speaking of which, I have a dog to send back and grass to mend." She clenches her fist, shattering the ice and the dog with it, before turning to look over her charred ground.

Sighing softly, she kneels down and closes her eyes, placing her palms flat on the charred earth. She murmurs a few unintelligible words, her thoughts and mind moving through the earth, seeking the roots, and energizing them by channeling her magic into them, feeling their fight as they push back up through the ground, reaching for the sky.

Zevran and Mordek watch her kneel and grow still, the grass growing at her fingertips and wrapping around her. They share a glance as they debate stepping in, but opt to wait. As time passes, they can feel the magic surrounding the clearing, watching the new shoots sprout and replace the charred ground from the Hellhounds.

Zevran mutters under his breath. "No wonder she tamed the nightshades in the kitchen."

"Which was scary enough. She could tame all of Hell's gardens with that power if she put her mind to it." Mordek replies.

Ten minutes later, Zadie opens her eyes, scanning the lush landscape once more. "There. All fixed." She rises and brushes off her dress, turning to Zevran and Mordek standing and staring in awe. "What, never seen a nature witch grow plants before?"

"Not like that, Zadie. Usually you plant seeds, water them and wait for them to grow."

"Yes, well, that's the long way. I have no desire to look at this shitshow and be reminded of your father."

"So, nature witch and elemental witch? Anything else I should know?"

"Well, the elements are a part of nature, so it's one and the same, and not that I know of. Now, if you don't mind, I am exhausted. Magic like that is draining, and I need to sleep. Thank you for the wonderful date." She gives a nod to Mordek. "Thank you both for helping. Have a good night." Turning, she walks back into her house and closes the door, flipping the lock behind her.

Glancing at Soot, she shakes her head. "Not discussing it. I am going to calm the nightshades down and crash." She marches into the kitchen, narrowing her eyes at the plants still screaming. "Alright, Beastlies! That's enough. I appreciate the warning about trespassers, but they are gone. How about tomorrow, I'll give you some sweet milk?"

She reaches out to pet them, hearing their screams dim to a hiss as they rustle their leaves and lean towards her, each earning a soft caress. "There. That's better. I will see you in the morning." Turning, she heads to the bathroom, going through her nightly routine before stumbling to bed.

Mordek eyes the closed door. "Well, damn. Guess I am sleeping in the greenhouse tonight."

"Looks like it. I guess I am heading to the castle to have some words with Daddy."

"Good luck with that."

Chapter Sixteen

Defying the Throne

Zevran phases back into Hell, his eyes blazing as he stares at the castle before him. Striding through the front gates, he ignores the other demons lingering there, the constants, always showing support for the family, or secretly wanting to tear them down, each hoping to get the inside track on their family. Turning, he spots his little sister running out a side door, launching onto him and wrapping her arms around his neck. "Lucilla!"

"Zevran! I heard you brought a mortal to the castle, one that got into a fight with Father."

Zevran chuckles and spins her around before placing her on her feet. "Indeed. She's my mate, and she's a fireball."

"Father is not happy. He's been ranting about it."

"Yes, well, neither am I. He sent Hellhounds to kill her."

"He what? Why?"

"You know Father's views on mortals."

"Yes, but if she's your mate, he should respect that. Mates are so rare."

"Exactly. So, I am heading upstairs to have a talk."

"Stop by the kitchens. Chef Ramone prepared your favorite."

"You're doing I assume?"

"Of course. Dad is raging. Figured you would need the buff Emberfruit grants you."

"Ah, yes. Nothing like fire in my blood before dealing with him."

She rises on her tiptoes and kisses his cheek. "Good luck, and I want to meet her! Especially if she's already caused this much chaos!"

"Once this settles down, I will take you to her."

"Perfect."

Zevran kisses her forehead and heads in the side door she just vacated, navigating his way to the kitchens. There on the counter is a dish, which what mortals would call, a blackened pomegranate, with glowing, ember red seeds. He stops and grabs a slice, taking a bite and closing his eyes as the fire floods his veins, stabilizing him. "Thanks Ramone. I needed this."

"For battling your father, yes."

"How does everyone know already?"

"Hellhounds talk. Said they were going to go kill the witch. Since all twelve returned in stasis, it's easy to deduce they failed. Your father's expecting you."

"Good." Zevran finishes the fruit and rises, giving a nod to Ramone. "Thank you for that." With that, he turns and leaves the kitchens, heading upstairs to his father's office. Stepping inside, he glances around at the destruction, and at his father, standing, staring out the window. "Well, well, well. What's the matter, Father? Did a mortal outplay you again?"

"I don't want you seeing her again."

"I don't care what you want. She is my mate."

Draemorr turns slowly, his eyes blazing as power radiates out from him. "No, she's not. Humans are not mates. It's not within their makeup. So stop this rebellion and pick a proper match."

"She is not just a human. She's a witch, with enough power to defeat the Hellhounds you sent to kill her…. Father." Zevran's jaw ticks as his voice edges, rolling out his own power to match his father's.

"I guess we will find out when they wake up if it was all her, or if she had help."

"Oh, she did. I killed two of them, she killed the rest. Just so you are aware, I will protect her at all costs."

Draemorr grins, a wicked delight flickering through his gaze. "You can't if you can't return to the mortal realm."

"What's that supposed to mean?" Zevran asks.

"It means, the second I felt you back in this realm, I closed your access back and forth. You are no longer able to cross back to the mortal realm."

"You can't do that."

"I AM THE KING! I can do whatever the hell I want." Draemorr roars, "Your witch disrespected me in front of the populace. I will not allow her to live."

"No... You disrespected yourself by sending a fireball at her. She simply defended herself and embarrassed you. That's what this is about, isn't it? That a mere mortal reflected your spell. Something you didn't expect from her, or any mortal for that matter. You do know witches exist right, and while some have no power, Zadie clearly does, enough so, she challenged you and came out on top." Zevran laughs at his father's expression, knowing if eyes could pop out, his would.

"You will marry Veyra at the end of the week. There is no choice in this matter. I have been patient enough. This is my decree, and I will announce it tomorrow at midnight."

"That sniveling, treasonous snake that runs to you with all the information she has? I think not. The ONLY one I will marry is Zadie."

"She is not a demon, and you can't marry the dead."

"She's not dead."

"Not yet, but she will be by the time you marry Veyra."

Zevran narrows his eyes on his father. "What did Veyra promise you, Father, because it had to be something?"

"She is a good match. Stunning, beautiful. Her father supports this, and it will bind our lineage together. She is politically useful and perfect for the next in line for the throne."

"Like you will ever step down. Does she know that? Did you tell her she would never be queen? That's what she wants. She's always played the game to achieve it so if she's so perfect, perhaps you should marry her. Gain your precious alliance and leave me to Zadie."

"You will not marry a mortal."

"Yes, I will. You told me it was high time to settle down. To be respectable. I have ALWAYS been the model son. Not chasing skirts like Talaris, nor picking fights like Drewgare, fights you have to keep sweeping under the rug. Or even my sister, Eryndria, who takes after Talaris, but on a much quieter level. I have kept my name out of the tabloids and given you as little grief as I can. But when I decide to stand my ground, you object. Zadie is my mate. And I WILL NOT give her up."

"I am sorry to have to do this, son, but that is not an option. You are hereby bound to the castle and its immediate grounds. At the end of the week, you will marry Veyra and forget about your mortal. If her soul arrives here, she will be bound to the Gallows tree so there will be no distractions in your marriage."

Zevran growls deeply, launching himself at his father, his claws extending as they swipe at him, only to feel himself yanked back and bound. "What the hell? This is not your power."

"No, it's not. It's Malacia's. I expected you and I would not see eye to eye."

"Who the fuck is that?" Zevran channels his own powers, trying to break the bindings holding him in place.

A sorceress steps out from the next room, weaving magic in her hands and wrapping it around him, moving to stand next to his father. Dressed in black and red robes, with sigils and barbed wire wrapped around her. Her black hair frames her dusky face, the tips writhing as if they are alive. Dark chocolate eyes stare back at him. "What do you want me to do with him?"

"Lock him in his room. I will need him bound again for his wedding night in a week."

"I can seal him in the room easily enough. I will need to return daily to reinforce it. His power is strong. He almost broke free."

"He is my firstborn."

"I understand, Sire." She lifts Zevran up, floating him behind the pair, and follows Draemorr, winding through the castle hallways until they come to a set of rooms. Stepping inside, she floats him over to his bed, and binds him down. Working her way through the suite, she ensures the wards are still active, strengthening them now that she understands the power she is working with. Once she's finished, she states. "It's good. He will not be leaving his chambers."

"Good. Thank you."

They both step out of the room, closing the door behind them, where Malacia seals it shut before they head back to Draemorr's office to discuss what needs to happen over the next few days.

Zevran feels the magic binds fade and rises, moving to the door and yanking on it. Feeling the resistance, he focuses inward, trying to fade out, finding himself bounced back into the room harshly, ending up flat on his back. Groaning, he pushes himself up, cursing inwardly at having walked into a trap. "Thane?"

Silence follows his question.

"Pyrrh? Nicx?"

More silence.

"Fuck!" Zevran stumbles to his feet. "If you guys can hear me, someone needs to warn Mordek who is watching Zadie!"

Chapter Seventeen

Destabilizing

Zadie wakes up late the next morning, staring at the ceiling in her room, a sense of dread creeping beneath her skin. She rubs her arms, trying to quell the prickle on her skin, sensing outwardly for her wards, still feeling them in place. Sighing, she pushes herself out of bed and pads to the bathroom, jumping as her cup flies off the counter. "What the hell?"

Picking it up, she places it back, seeing it rock back and forth before settling. Narrowing her eyes, she glances around, having intended to have a shower first, but thinking it might be best to expand her wards. She pads out to the kitchen, smiling at the nightshades in the windowsill, rustling and hissing softly at her presence. "Good morning, my little Beastlies. I need to expand my protection wards. Then I will give you the sweet milk I promised last night."

Behind her, her hanging pots clang against each other, causing her to jump and spin. She lifts a hand, stilling the gust of wind running through her kitchen, muttering softly as she scans for magic. "Something weird is going on."

Stepping outside, Mordek greets her, growling softly. "Why are you growling?"

"Making me sleep in the greenhouse, Lass. That's not very hospitable of you."

"Oh please. Do demons even sleep?"

"Besides the point. I am here to guard you, and you locked me out."

"Why didn't you just phase in?"

"Can't. Your wards are too strong."

"Well then, you will be pleased. I am expanding my wards to include the greenhouse and my surrounding yard."

"Right now?"

"Yes, there are strange things happening inside. I need to get them up pronto."

"Mind if I check the house?"

"Knock yourself out. This is going to take me a few hours." She starts at the edges of the house, calling forth the crystal embedded in the earth. Picking it up, she paces outwards sixty feet. Placing the dirt-encrusted crystal on the ground, she sinks it into the earth, murmuring a few words of warning "Circle strong, crystal bright, guard my home from those of spite." She repeats the process, taking two hours to expand her ring, and adding extra crystals in between the gaps. Pleased with her process, she brushes her hands off and returns to her house.

Stepping inside, she spies Mordek staring at the nightshades in the window. "Are you talking to my Beastlies?"

"No, I was just curious about how you tamed them. They still snap at my fingers."

"Well, perhaps if you treated them more as creatures than pests, they might like you."

"I do not do that."

"Really?" Zadie arches her brow and moves to the sink to wash her hands. "I recall Zevran calling them weeds."

"They are weeds, Zadie."

"Exactly my point." She dries her hands on the nearby dish towel and reaches out to caress them. "They are living. Therefore, they have thoughts and emotions. They might be more feral and incapable of processing like us, but they have enough to comprehend some things. Like sweet milk, and the hand that takes care of them."

Their leaves rustle as a few chirps escape the plants, before settling into a quivering hum.

"See, they know what sweet milk is. They recognize my voice. Treat them with respect, get respect back. Speaking of, are you following me to the store?"

"Of course. Zevran said not to leave you alone."

"How did his talk with Daddy Dearest go?"

Mordek frowns. "I don't know. I haven't heard from him. I thought he would check in by now."

"Perhaps they are still fighting. Time flows differently down there, does it not?"

"A bit, but enough time has passed that he should have reported in."

"Can you go check on him?"

"I can."

Exasperated, Zadie motions with her hands. "So go!"

"No can do. I made a vow to stay by your side."

"Fine. Is there a way to check in?"

"Not at the moment. But Thane should replace me this evening. I will find out more then."

"Wait, it's not just you watching me?"

Mordek laughs. "It's 90% me. He just has others step in when I am called back for meetings. Last time, Nicx covered you. Zevran doesn't want Daddy knowing I am here, so I still need to attend those."

"I see."

"They are going to be shocked when they can't phase into the yard anymore."

"Well, let me know and I can invite them in."

"I will."

"Thanks." Zadie sets about working in her kitchen, making the sweet milk that she promised them. Once it's finished, she stuffs it in the freezer for a few minutes to cool it off enough. Pulling a spoon out, she carefully pours some at each of their bases, watching the plants vibrate and hum in delight.

"They really like that, huh?"

"They seem to. Now, I need a shower, and then I have to head out to get food and mail packages."

An hour later, she pulls up at the shopping mall, watching a grocery cart roll across the parking lot and slam into a car. Sighing, she glances over at the passenger seat, seeing the familiar red eyes watching her. "I am guessing you are coming in."

Seeing what appears to be a nod, she grabs her purse and vacates the car. Moving to her trunk, she pulls out her reusable bags and her parcels. Double-checking her keys are in hand, she locks it up and walks across the lot. Stepping inside the mall, her gaze turns to a gasp, followed by a curse, spotting a person staring at the floor, coffee flooding from a cup on its side.

"Oh, coffee abuse."

The woman looks up at Zadie's comment. "I know, right? It's like it jumped out of my hand. Now I have to get another one."

"Sorry."

"It's just one of those days, I guess."

"I guess so." Zadie watches the woman turn back into the coffee shop and continues on her way. Stepping into the grocery store, she heads straight to the back, wanting to mail her orders out first. Hearing a crash behind her, she turns, seeing a few cans rolling around on the ground. "What the?"

Walking back, she picks them up and looks them over, placing them on the shelves, staring at them, trying to determine if there is a magical aura on them. "Are you doing this, Mordek?"

A quiet voice whispers beside her. "Not me. I watched them jump off the shelves, though."

She nods, hesitating a moment, before spinning and continuing to the post office. Standing in line, she sets her parcels down and waits, her eyes drifting over the people ahead of her. Feeling anxious, she sidesteps to the wall beside her, looking over the mailing packages. Picking one up, she turns it over, debating its size and what can fit into it. Hearing a groan from the man in front of her, she turns sharply and drops the box, trying to catch the guy falling over but struggling with his weight. Helping him, she lays the man down, resting a hand on his forehead. "Sir?"

Another woman from the front of the line, jumps in. "What happened?"

"I don't know. I was looking at the packaging, and heard a groan. Then he toppled my way."

"I'll call the emergency number!" She turns to the clerk as she pulls out her phone and dials. "You! Get your manager here."

Zadie nods, remaining at the man's side until store personnel arrive. Once they take over, she rises and steps back, moving over into the line that shifted. After she mails her parcels, she lingers in case they have more questions. Once the EMTs arrive, they question what happened, and she explains her side, giving them her contact information. "Is he going to be alright?"

"Hard to say. His blood pressure is really low, which is likely the cause of his passing out. But what's making it that way is what the doctors will find out."

"I hope he's alright."

"From what I understand, he's already better than he could be. If he smashed his head, he could be far worse, and you stopped that from happening."

"Only because he was collapsing towards me. Otherwise, I wouldn't have caught him in time."

"Good on you and your reaction time."

"Thank you." Zadie shakes their hand, wanting to get her groceries done and get home. As she makes her way through the aisles, more strange things happen, from a few soda bottles bursting, and bags of chips popping, one after the other, like firecrackers. She weaves around shopping carts that seem to have a mind of their own and apples rolling around on the floor from a collapsed display.

Quickly gathering a few things, she stands in line, her eyes lifting to the overhead lights flickering wildly, the buzz emanating from them growing louder until one bursts, earning screams from the people beneath it. She bounces on the balls of her feet, mentally urging the clerk to stop ogling the broken glass and start scanning. The quicker she can get out of here, the better.

When her turn arrives, she watches the clerk scan her items, opting to help and pack her bags herself. As she is stuffing the item in, a woman in the line next to her sinks to the ground. Averting her eyes, she pays for her food, grabs her bags and runs back to her car. Stuffing them into the trunk, she slides into the driver's seat, and rests her head on the steering wheel.

"Is it always that chaotic around you?"

"No, it never is. It's only that way when I am close to someone I care about."

"Aww, are you saying you care about me, Zadie? Wait till Zevran hears!"

"Mordek! That's not what I mean."

"Hey, don't stress. Whatever it is, we will figure it out. In all honesty, what was happening in there is more Zevran's curse; well, perhaps not curse, like your curse. Strange phenomena surround him. I wonder if, because you are his mate, you are channeling him somehow."

"Well, it can stop. I want to shop in peace."

"I will ask him about it."

Zadie starts the car and backs out of the stall. Driving away, she glances in the rearview mirror, seeing a loaded grocery cart following her, and behind that, a woman yelling and chasing it. As she stops to turn left, she sees the woman grab it and drag it back to her car. "Yes, something odd is happening."

She drives in silence, mulling things over in her thoughts. Was she channeling Zevran? Was it because they had seen each other over three times and he's still alive? Is it something else completely? There is only one other person she can ask, or rather, a cat. Soot. She sighs softly. Seeing her turnoff, she pulls onto her dirt driveway and parks, hopping out and collecting her bags. Stepping into the house, she calls out as she heads to the kitchen. "SOOT!"

A minute later, Soot pads into the kitchen and launches himself onto the counter, sitting with his tail hanging over the edge, twitching slightly. "Zadie? Why do you look frazzled?"

"Because I am Soot! Things happened at the mall. Strange things. It's been happening here too, actually."

"Yes, I've noticed."

"Well, what is it?"

"The energy around your curse is growing more chaotic because it recognizes Zevran as its match."

"And?"

"It means, Zadie, that your curse is destabilizing without him nearby. He's actually a magical grounding force."

She rubs her temples. "People are collapsing, Soot! Not just the ones I love."

"I realize that, Zadie. You need to accept Zevran fully. Embrace him as yours."

"I can't yet. I just..." She shakes her head, not wanting to accept what is right in front of her. Running from the kitchen, she heads to the bedroom, collapsing on her bed.

Soot watches her go, feeling the struggle in her mind. When Mordek moves to follow, Soot stops him. "Don't. She needs time. We have bigger problems."

Mordek hesitates, turning back to the cat. "What problems?"

"First. Someone needs to put this fridge and freezer food away, and since I don't have hands, that leaves it up to you."

"Fine. Elite warrior, delegated to groceries." Mordek mutters as he empties the bags, stacking the dry foods on the table and putting all the cold stuff away. "Happy?"

"Yes. When is your replacement coming?"

"Tonight sometime. Why?"

"According to the prophets, Draemorr has locked Zevran in his room. His father plans to have him wed by the end of the week under the blood moon."

"What?" Mordek hisses softly. "Clearly not to her."

"No, and Zadie can't know until the wedding day. It's going to be hard to stop her from seeing the tabloids. I might have to magically change the words on her screen."

"Why? And for what purpose?"

"Because that's when the prophets see her arriving. Besides, she has something to face here first this week."

"What's that?"

"Her past. You will know more when it happens since you will be here for it."

"How do you know all this?"

"I am her familiar. And I surf the supernatural web. Though this information came from a few chosen friends who want to see Zadie win."

"Win?"

Soot licks his paw and runs it over his ear carefully. "Yep, win."

"Damn, you are as cryptic as the prophets."

"That's what being a familiar is. The other part is curling up with my witch when she needs me, which is right now." He jumps off the counter and pads to the bedroom, where he launches onto the bed and weasels his way into her arms, purring softly.

***

After dinner, Mordek meets Thane outside the protected ring, who confirms the information Soot relayed to him. "What are we going to do, Mordek?"

"Up here, we pretend it's a normal day. Zadie can't know yet. Her cat has a plan."

"I won't say anything. Besides, she doesn't talk to me like she does you."

"Have you tried?"

"Ahh..."

"Exactly. She likes your voice."

"What?"

"Yes, she called it a book boyfriend voice."

"A book boyfriend? Isn't she Zevran's mate?"

"She is, but she clearly reads romance. You have the perfect voice. Try talking to her."

"That's great except I can't even get close to the house."

"Hold on..." He phases into the house to ask. "Zadie, be a dear and open a door for Thane."

Zadie sighs and places the book down. Crawling out of bed, she pads to the front door, seeing Mordek once again standing with Thane outside her protected ring. She straightens her pajamas and crosses the grass barefoot. Murmuring a few words, she mimes a door in the shield and opens it.

Thane glances between Mordek and Zadie, and steps through the door. "How can he pass without this door?"

"Because I allowed him in when I cast my spell. Him and Zevran."

"Wait, and you didn't allow me."

"Nope. You don't normally talk to me." She closes the invisible door, turns and heads back to the house.

Thane grumbles softly. "She's in a mood."

Mordek laughs, "You're lucky. At least you can access the house now. I had to stay outside in the greenhouse."

"Great. Do I even want to be in the house?"

"Probably not, but it's more comfortable. She will hide out in her room, which is off limits anyhow."

"Got it. See you when you get back."

***

Zadie wakes up the next morning and wanders into the living room, seeing Thane sitting on the couch reading. She gives a nod of greeting and makes her way into the kitchen, setting about brewing her tea and popping bread into the toaster. Once they're ready, she pours herself a cup and lathers peanut butter on the toast. She sits at her table, munching away as she watches the nightshades sway in the window to the beat of the pouring rain on the roof. A smile tips her lips, fully admitting to herself that she loves the little beastlies, more than any other plant she has owned.

Rising, she grabs her tea and moves to the window, petting each of them gently, thinking the weather is a sure sign to stay inside. Carrying her cup into the living room, she hesitates at Thane, suspecting she should say something to him only to notice the avoidance tactic of lifting his book and lowering his eyes. Opting not to press the issue, she moves to her computer and quickly checks her orders. Finding none, she continues to her bedroom and closes the door after her.

Perhaps a day of lounging in pajamas and reading will do her good. Picking up her book from her nightstand, she stacks the pillows and crawls back into bed, hoping to get lost in Emmaline's Escape, by N. Peterman. Her fingers caress the cover that caught her attention in the bookstore. A red-haired girl standing before a glowing doorway, the castle and lands beyond promising adventure... and according to the blurb, a chance to escape the marriage arranged for her by those who scorn her vitiligo. Cracking it open, she drifts away from her room and into the world of Tierra.

Chapter Eighteen

Interference

Back in Hell, the air is tense as Mordek enters the castle, searching for the other Ashen-Guards and finding them in the barracks. "What are you doing here?"

"We have been pulled off duty."

"What do you mean?"

Nicx shrugs. "It seems the King feels we are not needed at the moment."

"Let's phase to the silent peaks."

The nod and all slip into the between realm where few ears linger. Stepping onto a remote mountaintop, they gather around. "What's really happening?"

"The king has brought in a sorcerer or wizard. She's bound Zevran in his room. None of us can get past the spell, not even telepathically." Nicx paces over and stops to stare out over the horizon.

"The king plans on marrying him to Veyra," Pyrrh mutters. "Fucking snake. She is the one who warned the king of Zevran's mate. Been plotting to land him for far too long and now it looks like she's succeeding."

Skarix shakes his head. "No, we can't let him. Perhaps we can take out the mage?"

"Whose mage is it?" Mordek asks.

"Take a guess." Nicx mutters.

"Fuck, Veyra's?"

"Ding, ding. Mordek wins the prize." Skarix taunts.

"Her sister, actually." Pyrrh replies.

Mordek rolls his eyes. "Alright. Have any plans been made to free him?"

"And go against the King. Do you have a death wish?"

He chuckles. "I might, since I already know there is a plan in motion by Zadie's familiar. I will see if I can get a message to Zevran to sit tight. There is no way he is marrying that bitch Veyra. After this, she needs to go missing."

"Deal."

"Now, I need to know, is anyone going into his room? Like food services, siblings?"

"The chef is cooking him dinner. Otherwise, no, we have seen no one but the mage near his room, chanting. I hope she's not brainwashing him because if she is, she's dying next."

Pyrrh shakes his head. "Not that I can tell. It's keeping the wards up. Zevran is fighting them, and he's stronger than the mage expected."

"Good. Now, I need to get a message to him. I need him to be compliant so they have less guarding around him."

"What do you need?"

"I am not sure yet, but I will leave messages in our usual spot."

"Got it."

"Now, we should all filter back at random times. Two of you get to the dome and practice. We can't have it look like we are plotting."

"Right, I will go to the market."

"And I am going to talk with Chef Ramone."

"Good luck, Mordek. I think we are going to need it for this one."

"I have a witch and her cat in my back pocket. We got this." He winks and phases back to the castle where he left from. Leaving the barracks, he makes his way to the kitchen and steps in, his eyes landing on demons bustling around, clearly prepping for something. "Chef, can we talk?"

Ramone looks up and shakes his head, sending a slight nod towards the other door. "Too busy."

"I understand. I was just wondering if you had fire-hive honey?"

"Of course, I always have it. It's in the container over there."

Mordek moves over and lifts the lid, eyeing the flame-red honey. Grabbing a nearby bowl, he scoops a few spoonfuls into it and replaces the lid. Finding a smaller spoon, he thanks Ramone and heads into the eating area. Sitting down, he waits, twisting the spoon in his honey, until a message appears. *Lucilla wants to speak with you in the gardens.*

Mordek finally eats the honey, savoring each bite, before rising. He phases from the room and into the gardens, flitting through the plants until he finds Lucilla sitting at the base of a statue of a fallen angel, one wing broken, its shattered fragments still on the ground surrounding it. Her hands reach outward, as if pleading for someone to help, a look of pain etched on her face.

He approaches with caution, keeping to the shadows. "Princess Lucilla."

"Mordek. Were you followed?"

"No."

She lifts her hand, drawing a bubble over the two of them. Once it's secure, she turns to him. "What are you doing about my father?"

"What do you mean, Princess?"

"He's forcing Zevran to marry Veyra, who's not even his mate. I heard all about her at the ball and I already like her a lot, even if I haven't met her. That's who he should be marrying. If he's doing this to Zevran, I can just imagine what he's going to do to the rest of us."

"We are working on it, and it's best if you don't know so you can plead deniability. I need a message passed to him, though. Can you do that?"

"I can. Daddy knows Zevran is my favorite brother. He won't deny me a visit."

"Good. Tell him to comply. To stop fighting this."

"What? NO."

"Look Lucilla. If he keeps fighting, the King will have extra guards, and not us since he benched us. We need him to believe Zevran has accepted his fate, and not have extra reinforcements around."

"I understand."

"Just make sure no one gets the message but him. I suspect the mage has ears listening in on the room."

"I will. I think I might take up an old pastime with Zevran, and read a book with him."

"A book?"

"Yes, I always trail my finger along the words as I read, and stop on the one that matters, eventually forming the message I wanted to pass, without ever saying anything. I think it drove Dad nuts, but he never figured it out."

"Clever indeed. Now I need to return to the mortal realm. The King has already sent Hellhounds to kill Zadie. I hate to think of what's next. Hopefully, if Zevran agrees to marry Veyra, the King will stop trying to kill her."

"Good point. I never thought of it that way."

"Just be careful."

"I will. Thank you."

Mordek gives a nod and phases away, leaving her in the garden to ponder her thoughts. Arriving back at the house, he spots Thane on the couch and the bedroom door closed. "Anything happen?"

"Nope, she's locked herself in her room."

"Alright, I will take it from here." He lowers his voice to a whisper. "Our sector of the Ashen-Guards has been disbanded. Enjoy your time off."

Thane rolls his eyes. "Perhaps I might see what mortals have to offer."

"Just hide the horns."

Chuckling, Thane phases away, leaving Mordek alone, who makes himself at home on the couch.

***

Lucilla drops her shield and pads back into the castle, heading straight for her father's study. Pushing the door open, she glares at the mage and turns to her father. "I want to see Zevran."

"That's not a good idea, Lucilla."

"I don't care if it's a good idea. Someone needs to talk to him."

"He's throwing a tantrum, and no one is seeing him until he calms down."

Lucilla pouts her lips and widens her eyes, grabbing a strand of hair at the side of her face. "What if I can make him comply? You know that he and I always got along the best. Please, Daddy. I can feel his pain as if it's my own, and he always used to listen to me."

Draemorr stares at his daughter, feeling himself caving at her doe eyes. "Fine, see what you can do."

"Thank you, Daddy." She runs around the desk and wraps her arms around him, kissing his cheek.

"Yes, yes, don't thank me yet. Especially when Zevran throws you from his room, literally."

"He won't. I'm the one he likes!"

"True. The two of you were peas in a pod. I will have Malacia open a door into his room for you." He rises and takes her hand, gesturing for his mage to follow. At Zevran's suite, he nods. "Alright. Let her in."

"Are you sure this is wise?"

"She's been warned."

Lucilla glares at her. "He's my brother. He will not hurt me. You, on the other hand, I get it. If you locked me in my room, I would want to kill you too."

"Lucilla! Enough. I am only allowing you in to see if you can change his mind." Draemorr growls, power rolling off him.

"I know, Daddy. But who is she to question whether it's wise to see my brother?"

"She's Zevran's fiancée's sister."

"Oh, I see."

"You have one hour. Then Malacia will pull you out."

"I will make you proud, Daddy."

"No scheming, Lucilla. If I find out, you will be grounded and married to one of my choosing as well."

"I won't, Daddy."

Malacia chants a few words and creates a box around Lucilla at Zevran's door, lifting the wall and allowing her access. After Lucilla steps inside, she glances at the King. "She's planning something."

"Indeed, she is. Watch her."

Lucilla steps inside, taking in the trashed room, from shredded fabrics to broken porcelain. She drifts her eyes to the toppled bookshelves, with papers strewn all over, hoping at least one of them is intact enough to read. "Zev? What have you done?"

Zevran spins, his copper eyes glittering in anger. "Get out, Lucilla!"

She pouts, tilting her head to the side as she moves to the bookshelves. "Is that any way to talk to your most favorite sister ever!"

"I am not in the mood."

"Well, I am. I thought we might have some bonding time before your marriage. You know, like we used to when we read together."

"LEAVE, Lucilla!" Zevran growls, his eyes narrowing on his sister as he stalks forward, his claw extending in anger.

"I hope there is still something readable in here. You really have destroyed your suite." She squats down and rifles through the ones on the floor, picking up one with a black dragon on it. Dragonscales Divide. Flipping it over, she reads the back and rises, slamming into Zevran as she does. She runs her gaze up his body to meet his narrowed eyes, full of rage, and sends the tiniest wink his way. Stepping around him, she moves to the couch and pats the spot beside her. "It looks like you could use some calming time."

Fighting an internal battle, Zevran clenches his fists and strides towards what's left of his couch, sitting down beside his sister.

Once he sits down, she shifts over and curls up against him like when they were younger. Cracking open the book, she reads out loud softly, letting her fingers linger on certain words, spelling out a message to him as they did when they were younger.

Frustration I get Try to play nice Ash warriors fighting back but bound mission snow floral humans resistance ruler sitting in plush chair guard fight father human mate with them Compliance need to battle papa

She pauses in her reading and lifts her gaze to Zevran's for a moment, seeing that he is getting the message despite the disjointed words. "Are you feeling better?"

"I am. You picked a pretty good book."

"Well, we have to read fast, because Father only gave me an hour to calm you down."

Zevran chuckles. "He thought it would take an hour."

"I think longer actually, but I knew I could do it."

"I am glad you stopped by."

"Me too. You owe me!"

"For what!"

"For me being me!"

"Indeed." He wraps an arm around her and squeezes her shoulder. "Please continue. I want to know more about what happens to this shifter."

"Have you not read it already?"

"No. It was one of my more recent purchases."

She nods, her gaze straying momentarily towards the damaged books, and returns to reading, the two of them becoming lost in the story until the mage calls her back. As she steps outside. "I will see you at your wedding, Zev. Please don't destroy your room, or if you do, leave the books alone."

He chuckles. "I won't. I get it now. As the crown prince, there are certain things I need to accept, and this is one of them."

"Good."

With that, the seal is replaced, and Lucilla turns to her father. "You're welcome, Father. I still think it's wrong to lock him in like that." She turns and strides away, sending a dark look at Malacia, a smile slipping across her lips once she is out of sight.

Draemorr looks over at the mage. "Anything?"

"Nothing. No telepathic messages, no communication other than the initial fight and then their reading. I would like to see his book though, in case there are written messages in it."

Turning to the door, Draemorr projects his voice into the room. "Zevran, send that book out."

Smiling, Zevran picks up the book and slides it under the door. "Here you go. I want it back because I was enjoying it."

Malacia murmurs a few words on it and flips through it, shaking her head. "No magic here. It seems your daughter is right; she can calm the beast."

"She always has. Alright, give him the book back and let's get this planned."

Malacia transports the book back into the room and follows Draemorr back to his study, while Zevran moves to the bed and lies down, a smile crossing his lips at the thought of Zadie and whatever plans are being made.

Chapter Nineteen

Tabloids Altered

After spending a few days moping and hiding out in her room with Soot and a book, Zadie forces herself out of bed, knowing she needs to get her life back in order. Heading to the bathroom, she takes a refreshing shower, dresses and saunters into the living room, seeing Mordek has once again replaced Thane and is sitting on her couch. "Good morning, Mordek. Any news?"

"Apparently, he and his father fought until the wee hours of the night, and Zevran disappeared into his room. He is probably seething, and when he calms down, he will come see you. He doesn't want you to see his demonic side."

"How long does it usually take for him to calm down?"

"It depends on the rage level. By Friday, he should be calm enough to see you."

"Can you let me know if it's earlier?"

"I can, but I expect he will just show up."

"True. He has done that before." Zadie pads to the kitchen and starts her tea, listening to it hiss and percolate the water through. Moving to the nightshades, she caresses them gently. "Still high on sweet milk, I see. I did actually get more bones for you. I will work on them later." She laughs as they rustle their leaves and appear to do a happy dance. "Alright, Beastlies... Mordek, do you drink tea?"

"Of course."

"What do you take?"

"Two sugars if you have it, please."

"I do." Once the pot is full enough, she pulls it out, loving the fact that it auto stops and pours it into two mugs. Sliding it back in place, she scoops out two teaspoons into his and one into hers. Carrying them back to the living room, she hands him a cup and moves to her laptop, powering it on.

Mordek leans back on the couch, watching Zadie move around before settling on her computer. "What are you doing?"

"Looking to see if I have orders, or if any have gone missing."

"Does that happen often?"

"No. It used to be the people receiving the order, then saying they didn't get it. Then, I seek it with magic and find it in their house. Now they all know not to cross this witch. Even if the mail loses it, I can track it and see if I can get it back to its rightful owner."

"Interesting. It seems more trouble than it's worth."

Zadie laughs. "And being a Prince's guard is what? If that's not trouble with a capital T, what is?"

Mordek chuckles. "Except I am not the prince's guard right now. I am yours."

"Right, well. You don't pay my bills. This does. It puts a roof over my head, and so I send spells, potions, wands, through the mail to those who pay me money."

He nods and sips his tea. "I am sure that if you ask, Zevran can help."

"I am sure he can, but I enjoy crafting magical things. It spends some of my energy and calms me."

"Like fighting the training dummies does for me."

"Yes, I suppose." She grows silent as she takes down her orders, writing on the pad next to the computer. Once that's done, she skips to Supernatural Soulmates to see if Zevran emailed her. Sighing at the empty inbox, she tabs over to the tabloids, wanting to see if there is anything about the fight. Instead, she finds her date with Zevran all over it. "You know, the first thing I am going to do when I get back there is blow up the paparazzi."

"Why is that?"

"Just these tabloids. I don't even know how they found out about our date. It's not like when we were in Hell."

"What does it say?"

"Tiny Matchmaker Crashes Date. A little girl boldly proposed marriage to Hellion Royale in front of witnesses. His response? Perhaps a brother instead.

Did the Underworld's scion just admit to family plans? Has Snow Lily already melted the frozen heir's heart? There was only the child's family and their friends in that room with us."

"There are others that can spy like Ashen-Guard, Zadie. A lot of devils and demons phase. That's how we find those willing to sell their souls."

"I don't want to hear that."

Soot jumps on the desk, winds around the coffee cup and plants his butt down, purring softly. "Zadie, just take them with a grain of salt. It's the paparazzi."

"Have you read these, Soot?"

"Yes, some of them. I like the one talking about the Hellhounds. I think the title was, Snow Lily slays again."

Zadie rolls her eyes and scrolls down, skipping and finding the title, groaning at the words written there.

"Well, don't just groan. Demon over here, sitting on the couch, who wants to know. Read some out to me."

Zadie laughs. "I didn't know you were such a gossip hound."

"Oh, hell yes. We scroll through them all the time when on break. That's why there are so many of them."

"Aright, here are a few of them. Hellion Royale caught courting mortal flame? Spotted at the Coral Crown Restaurant, the King's notorious son (you know who)" Zadie pauses and rolls her eyes. "Notorious? Really?"

"Well, technically, he is the crown prince and would be notorious, just not in the way you are thinking. Please continue."

"Right... He was seen wining and dining the mysterious Snow Lily. Sources claim the two appeared alarmingly domestic, sharing food, laughter, and far too much eye contact for a casual dinner. Is the Underworld's most eligible bachelor finally off the market?" Zadie mutters beneath her breath. "Of course he is; he's my mate."

Soot bats at the pen on the desk, watching it roll across the pad and onto the floor. "He is, but have you accepted him yet?"

"It's complicated." She reaches down and picks up the pen, placing it on the other side, away from her cat.

"It's not that complicated, but we can discuss that after."

"I would rather not."

Mordek grins at her avoidance, "Alright then. I want the one your cat was talking about."

"Fine." She scrolls back to the article. "Snow Lily slays again. Literally! In a scandal that has Hell reeling, Snow Lily herself reportedly vanquished all twelve of the King's own hounds. The Hell Court has yet to comment, but whispers claim Daddy Dearest is seething. The question remains: is she the Underworld's greatest threat or its future Queen?"

"Yes, those are the juicy details I want. Anymore like that?"

Zadie reads through a few of them and stops. "Yes, one more... Beauty, beast, and betrayal? Snow Lily's rise has tongues wagging: from romantic dinners at the Coral Crown to scandalous victories in blood, she has captured not only the gaze of Hellion Royale but the ire of his father. One thing is certain. Hell hasn't seen headlines this juicy in centuries."

Mordek laughs. "I love it. You are taking Hell by storm, which is perfect since you are an elemental witch!"

"Gawd, you are just as bad as Soot!"

"Anymore?"

Zadie snaps her laptop shut. "No, I am not catering to your addiction! Neither of yours."

"What's the plan for today?"

"Roasting bones and probably a quick clean of the place."

"Mind if I join you?"

"You are going to clean?"

Mordek chuckles. "Hey, I have my place that I clean in Hell, and we get a lot more ash than you do. I meant the roasting bones part."

"Are you going to tattle again about my cooking?"

"No. Now that I know the plants will not rage and eat you, there is no need."

Zadie laughs softly, reaching out to pet Soot. "I see. I appreciate you asking, especially since I know you were joining anyway, and I would love to see you clean!"

"Of course you would," Mordek mutters softly. "Besides, Zevran said not to leave your side, so if that includes gardening, roasting, or cleaning, then that's what I do."

"Alright. Well, bones first. The nightshades have a patience problem, but they are getting better."

"You think?"

"Hey, be nice. Or I will sic them on you."

"I am sure you would, and with the way they are around you, they would listen."

"Of course they would. First though, I need food, then we can get on with the day." Zadie rises and heads into the kitchen to make breakfast. Afterwards, she takes the bones out of the fridge, eyeing them carefully, knowing it's been a few days since she bought them. Sniffing them, she crinkles her nose, and holds one out to Mordek. "Do you think these are all right?"

"Yes, the more rotten, the better."

"Makes sense." She places them in a bowl and carries them out back to roast them. Setting them up, she leaves Mordek to turn them over as she tends to her plants, watering and pruning, setting a few herbs aside for dinner. When they are done, she carries them back into the plants, laughing at their antics in the windowsill, each leaning down to the bowl with soft hisses and squeals. "Hey, you keep doing that, you might topple your planter, Beastlies. Soon."

Mordek moves over to the other side, chuckling. "I never thought I would see the day."

"Well, you have, and Hell hasn't even frozen over."

"Not yet. Soon, I expect."

Zadie snaps her gaze up to Mordek. "What's that supposed to mean?"

"Nothing. Just a train of thought."

"What train of thought?"

Mordek sighs. "I was just thinking of you freezing the guards. That's all. Ones that are still frozen, in fact."

"Oh." She studies him, knowing instinctively he is keeping something from her. "Are you sure?"

"Yes. What did you want me to clean?"

"You can start in the living room."

"Got it." Mordek rummages under the sink and grabs some cleaning supplies, heading to the living room to clean.

Zadie's gaze follows him, thinking to press him, but the grumble of the nightshades draws her attention back. Sighing softly, she gets to work, grinding the bones and feeding them, before tackling the rest of the house. At the end of the day, she checks her emails hopefully, only to have her shoulders slump when there is nothing from Zevran.

Chapter Twenty

Fire Walks

Zadie opens her eyes and stares at the ceiling, feeling Soot pressed up against her, purring softly. She reaches out and runs her fingers over his silky fur, feeling the rumble of his chest. "Morning, Soot."

"Morning, my favorite witch. What's the plan today?"

"I need to head into town and pick up the bottles I ordered. After what happened last time at the market, I am hesitant to go, but I need them to complete orders. Especially since I am losing jars to breakage because of channeling the chaos energy. In fact, I am leery of even crafting potions right now with the magic surrounding me."

"Your magic is stronger than the chaos. If you need it, I can help with creating a grounding space."

"I just hope people don't collapse. I mean, cans falling, chips exploding, that's one thing, but it's affecting others; that's not good, Soot."

"It will be fine, Zadie. There is only one person there, right? You can send Mordek in with the cash to get them while you wait in the car."

"Right, I never thought of that."

"That's what I am here for. I come up with all the good ideas."

Zadie laughs, nudging her cat gently as she pushes the covers back. "I suppose I should get my ass in gear."

"Yes, you'd better."

She rolls out of bed and pads to the bathroom, getting a start to the day. An hour later, she walks out of her bedroom, seeing Mordek staring out the window. "Morning, Mordek."

"Good morning, Zadie."

"Have you heard anything?"

"Alas, no. Soon though, I hope. Rumor has it he trashed his room, so there is that."

"What?"

"Well, a rage will do that. Shredded clothes, bedding, a toppled bookshelf and ripped pages."

"He'd better not trash this cottage."

"He won't."

"And yet, he trashed his room."

"Yes, because it's his. That's why he is staying there. He won't willingly bring harm to your things."

"I guess you have a point."

"I do. What's on the agenda for us today, Zevran's Mate!"

Zadie laughs, "First, morning tea and food. Afterward, I need to head into town and fetch an order. If I gave you cash, do you think you could run in and get it? I don't want whatever this is surrounding me to hurt anyone else."

"I can do that."

"Thank you. Do you want tea? Food? I can make some bacon and eggs."

"That would be lovely."

Giving a nod, she heads into the kitchen and works on making breakfast. When it's done, she plates it and sets it on the kitchen table carefully, stopping the plates from skidding off at the last minute. "Damn, if this keeps up, I am going to need to buy a whole new set of dinnerware."

Mordek sits and grabs his plate firmly. "I got it."

"Thanks." She settles by hers, deftly catching her fork as it flies away from her. "Nice catch!"

Chuckling, she shakes her head. "Zevran and I are going to have a little talk about his magic. It's disturbing my life."

Soot pads into the kitchen, sniffing his bowl in disdain. "Kibble? Really?"

"You get meat tonight. It's always kibble in the morning."

"We really need to have meat in the morning too."

"Not happening, Soot."

"Fine, since you are intent on starving me, I am going to doom scroll on your computer." Sniffing the air, Soot lifts his head and prances out of the kitchen, leaving the pair to eat.

"Have fun."

Mordek arches his brow. "Doom scroll?"

"It's a mortal term where you scroll through what's on the web. Often, stories of death, doom and destruction. Soot has a fascination with it, especially since three of my ex's died."

"Is he trying to solve why?"

"Perhaps. I already know I am cursed."

Mordek feels the mood of the room change, reading the sadness suddenly flooding her eyes, the smile leaving her lips as she drops her eyes to her plate, pushing her food around. "Zadie, Zevran is not mortal, and he will help you figure it out."

"I know he says that..."

"He will. Trust me. He already loves you."

"Only because I am trouble in his life and his father hates me."

"That helps for sure." Mordek winks at her, grinning.

She laughs. "Alright. He loves me. No more talk of this. Eat your breakfast."

After enjoying breakfast, she washes the dishes and walks to the living room where Soot sits at her computer. Kissing the top of his head, she murmurs. "Don't look at too many Donskoys, or is it Bambinos?"

"Sphynx and someone clearly looked into cats on my behalf."

Zadie shrugs and grabs her car keys off the desk. "I need ammunition for when you mock me for reading romance novels. Why a Sphynx?"

"Because they are purrfect. The Donskoy's look perpetually cranky, and the Bambino's legs are too short."

"They look fierce, not cranky. And if you want long legs, the Peterbald has them, but if I have the choice, I would take the elf cat. They look adorable. I wonder if they come in a familiar type variety."

"ZADIE! Don't you even think about that!"

Laughter escapes her as she leans down to kiss his head again. "I have the best one of the lot, and I wouldn't trade you for anything."

"Good." His tail twitches in agitation as he drops his paw on the scroll wheel of the mouse, turning his attention back to the monitors.

Zadie grabs her purse and heads out the front door to the car, sliding in the driver's seat as Mordek settles into the passenger seat. Starting the car, she backs it up and turns towards her driveway. "It's just one stop. I would leave it until shopping day, but I need bottles for my potions tomorrow since most of them broke last time you tattled and Zevran tried to stop me from feeding my beastlies."

"To be fair, the nightshades in Hell would rip you apart."

"Doubtful. Witch, remember?"

"There is that. Can they not deliver?"

"This far out? Nope. Not even the mail comes out here, so I have a lockbox in town."

"That's terrible."

"It's not so bad. It means I get peace and quiet from everyone out here. When Desmond self-imploded, our paparazzi were peering in my windows or lurking around my doors, testing them constantly to see if they could get in. Now, I am too far out for it to be worth their time. That and they would need to find me. I kind of crossed the country in a hurry."

"How much of a hurry."

"A magical one. I bought this place sight unseen on the witches' web. The witch who owned it, magically called me and my belongings to it. My place sold the same way a month later, and I believe a young witch lives there."

"I did not know."

"It's no different from your web."

"True."

Zadie continues into town, and pulls up and parks the car in front of the glassworks store, staring at all the products that can break if she enters. Pulling her purse onto her lap, she fishes out her money and hands it over to Mordek. "Here, the order is under Zadie. If they ask, just tell them, my car battery died, and I need to keep it running to charge it."

He accepts the money and shifts his appearance to hide his demonic heritage. Slipping out of the car, he makes his way into the store.

Zadie glances around as she waits, seeing others pulling in and getting out of their cars, while people mill about or wander the crosswalks, heading into the variety of stores nearby. Catching a flicker of movement in her rearview mirror, she lifts her gaze, gasping in shock at her ex, Desmond, standing there.

Spinning around in her seat, she looks out the back window, seeing a group of teenagers hanging out. She follows her gaze around the car before returning it to the rearview. Seeing nothing, she runs a hand through her white hair, jumping with a slight yelp as Mordek opens the passenger door.

"Zadie? Is everything alright?"

"You just scared me, that's all."

"Do you want these in the back seat?"

She leans down and pops the lever at her feet. "Trunk is good." She watches him place them in the back before returning to the seat.

Sliding in, he looks at her pale features. "Are you sure? You look pale."

"It's fine. I just thought I saw someone I knew."

"And that's a bad thing?"

"From my past, and yes. Thank you for getting the jars." She backs the car out of the lot and pulls back onto the road.

"You are welcome."

Zadie laughs at his comment.

"What?" Mordek asks.

"It's nothing, really. You know, we are raised here to believe that demons and devils are not to be trusted. The devil will steal your soul if you say or do the wrong thing. Don't trust them, for their words are tainted. That sort of thing, but overall, most of you are more polite than some humans I have met."

"I think it's the same in our realm, Zadie. We have the good and the bad. It's all about who you choose to surround yourself with."

"I get that." Zadie grows silent as she watches the road, her gaze darting to the rearview mirror more often than normal. Pulling onto her driveway, she slows the car over the gravel, careful not to jostle the jars in the back too much. As she rounds the corner just before her protection borders, she slams on the brake, staring at the man in her way. One she recognizes, and one that should be dead.

"Is that the person you think you saw, Zadie?" Mordek follows her gaze to the man standing in their way, taking in the unnatural eyes, the dark brown hair, glinting with hints of red as he turns his head. Decent enough body but covered in clothing that has seen better days.

Zadie's hands shake as she grips the steering wheel, her voice dropping to barely a whisper. "Yes."

"Who is he?"

"Desmond, my ex, who self-combusted."

"What? How?"

"I don't know."

Desmond places his hands on his hips, narrowing his eyes at the car. "Zadie Halovale. It's been a long time."

"Don't get out of the car, Zadie." Mordek slips from the passenger side and closes the door behind him. Facing Desmond. "You are not wanted here. Return from where you came."

Desmond quivers his hands and shakes his legs, maniacal laughter erupting from his chest. "Oohh, she has an Ashen-Guard protector. My knees are shaking, can you tell?" He lifts a hand and sends a stream of fire at the car, watching as the metal twists and screeches beneath the heat.

Zadie bites the scream back and flings her door open, she scrambles from the car as heat radiates from where she just sat. Growling softly at the destruction of her vehicle, she rises to her feet and brushes her jeans off, glaring at Desmond. "That was my car!"

"You will not need it after I get through with you."

"What do you want, Desmond? You're supposed to be dead!"

"Yes, and who KILLED me? You did. You knew the risk and didn't tell me. Do you think you are worth dying for? Because I can tell you, you are not."

"It's not like that."

Desmond clenches his fists and sweeps a hand in her direction, sending another wave of fire her way.

Zadie catches Mordek shifting into his demonic form as she brings up a wall, deflecting the flames intended to engulf her. Feeling the sting, she steps back, staring at him in horror that it made it through her witchcraft. Narrowing her eyes, she traces a few runes in the air, sending her own spell back, watching the ice hit him and erupt in a geyser of steaming water.

Mordek engages with Desmond, his claws raking through his skin, where instead of spilling blood, molten lava drips and scars the ground. "What the fuck?"

"Mordek, get out of there." Zadie draws on another spell, knowing if he's made of fire, he's immune to fire, not that her ice worked either. It melted before it reached him, which meant calling on larger effects, and that meant Mordek was bound to suffer.

"Zadie, I am..."

"Mordek, MOVE!" She weaves her hands, drawing on a larger rune, encasing it with fragments of ice and drawing the breeze from the air. It snapped and sparked before her, growing in size.

Seeing the size of the magic growing in front of her, Mordek darts back behind her, passing the rune on the way. He spins just as it explodes on contact with Desmond standing before him, knocking him back as snow and ice chunks surround him in a whirling tornado.

Lava seeps from Desmond's body as the shards slice through his skin. Desmond's eyes narrow, a roar escaping as flames rise and billow around him, ending Zadie's spell. He grins wickedly, and stalks forward, sending a blast of flame towards her.

Zadie steps back, muttering under her breath as her spell dissipates, drawing up a shield to protect herself, feeling the sting as some flames slip past it. "Oh. That's not good. If ice doesn't hurt fire, what else does?"

"Water?"

"Ice IS water, Mordek!"

"I mean a lot of water."

"That was a lot!"

"You have a lake out back, yes?"

"Yes."

"Let's go."

Zadie bolts away from Demond, mentally cursing her chunky heels on the soft ground, hearing his laughter echoing all around them in the woods. Seeing him flicker in front of them, she veers to the left as Mordek engages him, catching their growls, before feeling Mordek beside her again.

"Keep running. I injured his leg, but the lava within is healing him."

"Fuck, who the hell would do this?"

"I'd give you three guesses, but you only need one."

Zadie growls softly. "You know the paparazzi might be correct."

"Why's that?"

"There might be a new queen in town."

Mordek pushes Zadie to the right, watching her stumble to her knees, taking the burst of lava to his chest, intended for her. His claws lengthen again, this time aiming for Desmond's eyes, raking them across his face.

Desmond howls in rage and launches onto Mordek, dragging him to the ground. "RUN, ZADIE!"

Zadie staggers to her feet, her wrist throbbing where she landed on it, and beelines straight for the lake. Reaching the edge, she circles around to where the small dock sits.

Glancing back, she staggers down the wooden planks, her boots thudding softly as they creak under her weight. She jumps as Mordek reappears beside her, sporting several burns on his skin.

"He's on his way."

Zadie spins, fire flickering at the edge of the dock. Desmond reappears, his molten skin cracking and glowing, lava spilling through the seams of his flesh. His eyes burn like furnaces as he stalks towards her. "YOU killed me, Zadie. Now I will burn you."

Zadie stumbles back, murmuring a few words and wrapping a water-breathing spell through her body, just as Desmond lunges. She yelps in surprise as his molten hands lock on her wrists, the stench of burned skin assaulting her senses.

Determined to defeat him, she wraps her hands around his arms and hooks the heel of her boot on the edge of the dock. Pushing with all her strength, she launches them both backwards, tumbling into the depths of the lake. Cold water hisses and bubbles around her as she allows herself to sink deeper.

The lake seethes with steam, fish scattering in flashes of silver. Those too slow floating lifeless to the surface, boiled from the shockwave.

The water churns as Desmond thrashes, his molten body fighting the cold. Lava leaks from the cracks in his chest, cooling into jagged black rock, then breaking apart as more fire bursts free. He opens his mouth to roar, but water surges in. His body convulses, steam spewing from his jaws, pressure cracking through him as his hands tighten on Zadie.

The temperature rises around them. Zadie struggles to get away, panic flooding her at the thought of being boiled alive. She kicks against him, aiming hard between his legs, not knowing if his molten body even still carries such things. He jolts, his grip faltering enough, and she wrenches free just in time to see a blur cutting through the murk.

Mordek slams into Desmond, his claws sinking in deep and raking through his molten chest. A plume of fire bursts, only to be immediately snuffed and swallowed by the lake in a blast of steam.

Zadie yanks a few weeds from the bottom and caresses them in the water, strengthening their resistance to fire and bringing them to life. She releases them, watching them slither towards Desmond, latching around his legs and weaving with the ones still attached on the bottom, dragging him deeper. Knowing she needs to get Mordek out of there, she sends a tiny sigil with a message to him as she kicks her way to the surface and swims for shore.

Dragging herself through the waterlilies and weeds, she stumbles onto the solid ground, looking back at Mordek following her. Once he is out of the water, she nods and backs up, and sends a wall of force outwards, pushing the living creatures out with it. Once she's certain the area is clear, she chants again and creates a tiny pebble of ice. Flicking it into the water, she smiles as shards of ice streak from it, growing rapidly, freezing the water on this side of the invisible ice. The ground trembles beneath their feet, and Zadie reaches for Mordek to steady herself.

"What the hell's happening, Zadie?"

"Fire and Ice are about to go boom. We need to leave."

They turn to run, only to be thrown to the ground by the explosion behind them. Zadie covers her head as a mix of wood, water and ice rains down upon them. Once the air stills, she braves a glance behind her, finding nothing but blissful silence. "I think he's dead."

Mordek phases back to the lake, searching for any remnants and finding nothing. Returning to her side, he helps her to her feet. "He's gone."

Zadie rises, looking over the burns on her arms from his hands, and sighs, muttering angrily. "Fucker. And here I thought he was nice when I dated him. He did all the right things. Now I am glad he imploded." She looks back over the lake, seeing the destruction there. "He owes me a bloody dock! Now where am I supposed to sit and read in the summer?"

Mordek chuckles. "Come, we need to get you into dry clothes and get those burns wrapped up."

Zadie nods and follows Mordek home, her eyes drifting over to where her melted car sits. "And a new fucking car!"

"He's dead, Zadie, and I doubt his estate will cover it, especially if he died, what? How many years ago?"

"Oh, Desmond's not covering it. You're right. Fucking Daddy Dearest is! I think I will just take Zevran's car over there as collateral damage." She stomps into her house, heading straight to her bathroom. Twenty minutes later, after a shower and getting dressed in dry clothes, she carries her medical kit into the living room and settles on the couch next to Mordek, sitting patiently as he tends her wounds.

"Are you really alright, Zadie? No other wounds?"

"Nah, I feel like I have a sunburn all over my skin, but aloe will clear that by morning. Where he grabbed me will take a few days though."

"Good. Please tell Zevran I was here to protect you. He's going to go batshit crazy when he sees these."

"Don't worry, I've got your back."

"Thanks."

"Now, if you don't mind, I think I am going to curl up and watch a movie. I need to destress."

"Got it. I will be close by."

"Thanks, Mordek. I really appreciate your help today. I have never faced a creature as strong as him."

"Daddy went from hounds to the strongest he has. Those are last-line warriors. Him using Desmond meant he already had access to him."

"Yes, I figured that out."

Mordek places a reassuring hand on her shoulder and phases back to watch.

Zadie picks the remote up and clicks on her TV and navigates to her streaming services. Deciding on a movie, she drags a blanket over her and curls up, drifting more in thought than paying attention to what's on the screen. Wondering why Zevran didn't show up to help. Was his rage so bad that he couldn't sense her in trouble? If it was, did she really want to be tied to someone like that? A few tears slip past, creeping down her cheeks.

***

The next morning, Zadie wakes up, a stiffness permeating her frame. She groans when she realizes she fell asleep on the couch. All because she was moping that Zevran had not helped her yesterday. Well, no more. Today, she has things to do. Like making magical items for her customers. If he wants to throw a hissy fit, so be it. She is just going to return to life as she knew it. But first, an actual bath to get the kinks out.

Slipping from the couch with a groan, she smiles at Soot, curled up at her feet, and makes her way to the bathroom, spending an hour in the hot water. Feeling the aches subside, she steps out, dries off and dresses. Padding back into the living room, she goes to grab the keys from the rack, cursing at the fact that they are not there, recalling they are still in the ignition of the new hunk of metal sculpture just outside her protections. Sighing, she pushes the door open only to hear Mordek's voice.

"Where are you going, Zadie?"

"To get my jars, assuming there are any left."

"I will. I do not want you stepping past your protection."

"Fair enough. Thank you. If you can bring them to the kitchen, that would be great." After he phases out, she pads to the kitchen, stopping to greet her nightshades, their soft hisses and screams easing her anxiety.

Mordek returns a few minutes later with half a box of jars. "I left the others in the trunk."

"Better than none, I suppose. I will just order more later. Hey, question. Have you heard anything from Zevran?"

"No, I have not, but I have not traded guards since Thane was here. We can't just pick up a phone and call."

"True. Sorry, I didn't think about it."

"Hey, no, don't be sorry. Yesterday was stressful for you. I'm sure he has a good reason, and if he doesn't, just turn him over your knee and spank him."

"You are so bad, Mordek!" She laughs at the thought of the demon prince over her knee. Lifting her box of jars, she carries it back to her craft room, feeling Mordek on her heels.

"So this is your magic room."

"Yes, it's where the magic happens."

"Well, I will leave you to it. If you need anything, let me know."

"I will." Zadie attempts to craft orders, but after the first jar breaks, she decides perhaps another day. Leaving her stuff there, she makes her way out the kitchen door into the gardens. There she spends the afternoon puttering and tending to her plants, enjoying the peaceful calm it grants her, stopping only for lunch and dinner. After dinner, she curls up on the couch again, flipping through the movies and settling on one to watch with Soot.

Hellbound

Friday morning, Zadie mopes at her computer, tea in hand, skimming through the supernatural tabloids, growing accustomed to seeing her name all over their tabloids, searching for information on Zevran since she still hasn't heard from him. Her eyes narrow Mordek's way, knowing he is keeping secrets, with how evasive he's been, sticking to phase form to avoid conversations.

Especially after Desmond attacked two days ago. She would have thought, if anything, Zevran would have shown up. She drifts her gaze down to the bandages on her arms, burns from her fight and healing nicely considering how bad they were.

She chews on her lip, knowing it's been a week since he confronted Daddy and since she's seen him last. Something happened that day that her guards are remaining silent about. She can feel it in her bones. Perhaps she should look through her books and see if there is a truth spell there.

Flipping over to the supernatural web, her hand stills on the mouse, reading the words scrawled on her screen.

Infernal Alliance Sealed: Demon Prince's Engagement Announced by Royal Patriarch.

Opening the article, she reads the first few lines.

No word from the Prince himself, but his father insists the union will strengthen the bloodline. Eyewitnesses report Prince Zevran looked… less than thrilled. Talk about a shotgun wedding; only this one's loaded with brimstone. Speculation rises: is this duty, or defiance of the Prince's true affections?

Further down, she reads.

Chains Forged in Fire: Public Celebration Set for Demon Prince's Binding
The father extends an invitation to all. A union meant to unite realms or control them.

"Mordek!" Her eyes turn to her bookshelf, seeing his familiar red gaze. "Is this true?"

"Is what true?"

"Is Zevran engaged?"

"Yes. His father is using his power to force him."

"Why didn't you tell me?"

"He asked me not to. He knows you are hesitant about your relationship and doesn't want to force your decision."

"I am NOT hesitant about the relationship. Just the curse killing him and ending the world."

"SOOT!!"

Soot lifts his head from his nap, running a paw over his face. "What is it, Zadie?"

"Did you know?"

"Of course I did. There are a few good articles out there about his engagement and wedding all in one day. My favorite is the one that talks about what the prophets are saying. How did it go? Prophets whisper that a shadow will rise before the vows are sealed."

"And you didn't tell me either."

"Nope. I told you I was not pushing you."

Zadie rises and stalks over to the window, staring out at her yard, running a hand through her hair in agitation. "Who is he getting married to, Mordek?"

"A wealthy demon heiress. It's a political arrangement that gives his father more control."

"What's her name?"

"Veyra. She's the one that narked on the pair of you in the first place. I hate to tell you, but she is over the moon, telling everyone they are mates and that it's a match made in Hell... that sort of thing."

"What type of demon?"

"Succubus."

"What are their weaknesses?"

"Zadie..."

"No, Mordek. Either you tell me now, or I will find out the hard way."

"Ice. Most of us are vulnerable to it, but your fires are also dangerous to us. They will not expect that. Also holy magic. The type priests and paladins cast."

"I don't have that...Take me there, Mordek."

"I can't. Only royals can pass mortals through the barriers of Hell."

Zadie nods, growing thoughtful. "So I need someone who can."

"Zevran can't. His father bound him to Hell, and it's not likely his siblings will defy their father's orders to help you. They are not as defiant as your mate is yet."

"No, but one is rebellious. He is in the tabloids all the time."

"Talaris is more interested in the skirts he can get into."

"True, there is that, but that's not who I was thinking of. First, I need to get dressed. I mean, there's a party, and I wasn't invited." She strides into her bedroom, throwing open the closet doors like a queen choosing armor. Supple leather pants hug her legs as she slips into them, followed by a cropped purple top, the words *I Am the Storm* sprawled in bold defiance across her chest. A wide, chunky belt cinches at her hips, the metal gleam catching the light as she fastens it snug. Two-inch high buckled boots follow, heavy enough to stomp but stylish enough to strut. She slides knitted armbands up over the bandages, because she's pretty certain Daddy Dearest had something to do with Desmond and she doesn't want him to see the damage he caused.

At the dresser, she slips on several gold bangles, spinning them for a moment on her wrist. Then she lifts a black velvet choker; a deep violet band with a hematite stone glinting darkly at the center. Fingering it, she clasps it around her neck, a final note of rebellion and power. Satisfied, she pivots on her heel and saunters back into the living room, ready to crash a party that never wanted her.

Mordek runs his gaze down Zadie, seeing how perfectly the outfit suits her personality. "Damn, if that's not the epitome of a witchy human, I don't know what is."

"That's the point, Mordek." She turns and moves to her bookshelf, running a finger along the spines. Pulling one out, she caresses her fingers over the cover. "Right, I am going downstairs."

Soot jumps up from the couch. "Zadie. What are you doing?"

"I am going to call on a bit of aid." She strides through the kitchen, pausing at the nightshades, her fingers petting them as their leaves rustle in delight. "Guard my house, Beastlies. I have a prince to rescue." She turns and hesitates, looking back at the plants. "Beastlies. Could I have a petal, thorn or leaf? It would help."

They rustle amongst themselves and one of them sheds a black petal into her hand.

"Thank you." She closes her hand around it carefully. Pushing through the back door open, she heads to the cellar and opens it. Mordek and Soot trail after her as she descends into the dark, damp air. Snapping her fingers, candles flare alive in obedient waves, light chasing the shadows in the chamber until a soft glow fills it. In the center, carved into the stone floor, runes and sigils wind together into an intricate ring. Four half-burned candles, with wax remnants pooling at the base, sit evenly spaced around the circle.

"What is this?" Mordek asks warily.

"A summoning circle."

"What! Zadie, Zevran will not approve."

"Mordek, if you're going to bitch, go upstairs."

Soot saunters to a corner, jumps on top of a box, and curls up like he's settling in for a show. "Might as well settle in, Mordek. These can take hours."

"Wait... she's done this before?" Mordek blurts out.

"Why do you think there's a permanent circle carved into the floor?" Soot replies without batting an eye.

"Is it safe?"

"Not always; that's why the wards around the edges. Keeps the spirit confined."

Mordek sits on the box next to Soot, apprehension teeming within him. He had heard of mortals summoning creatures beyond their knowledge, often ending in their demise. Yet. Here Zadie was, doing so with confidence in every movement.

Zadie steps into the circle and kneels, setting the book within the marked square carved into the stone. Above it, she places the precious petal the nightshades granted her. The air stills as she flips through its pages, her fingertips tingling with heat and cold at once. She finds the passage she needs and murmurs softly. "Be this my circle. A sphere of protection and containment. None shall enter without my consent, nor shall they leave without it either. This is my will, and it shall be heard. So mote it be."

The runes blaze to life, fire-red at first, but streaked through with sudden threads of silver-white that dance like falling stars. A shimmering dome rises, its surface rippling between molten shadow and crystalline light, glistening like glitter in a bubble, before fading.

She sits in meditation as time passes, murmuring unintelligible chants under her breath, while flickers of light and shadow move within the circle. Eventually, Zadie lifts her chin and speaks, her voice ringing with authority. "I, Zadie Halovale, call forth Charognis, guardian and gatekeeper of Hell. I demand that he answer my call and hear what I have to say."

Mordek gasps in shock at who Zadie is attempting to summon. He leans over and whispers to Soot. "I doubt he will…"

Soot lifts a paw, his tail flicking in agitation. "Shhh, just watch."

She smiles as the circle remains empty, not surprised in the least. She straightens her shoulders, drawing on her power as a thrum fills the surrounding air. "Charognis. I know you heard me. Do NOT make me drag your three-headed, snake-ridden, furry ass here. Cross the realms now!"

Another few moments and the circle remains empty. "So be it. We will do this the hard way." She flips the pages and touches a few runes within the circle, each lighting up as she does. "I call upon my ancestors to help me. Cross the great divide and lend me your power."

Feeling a warmth envelop her, she watches the flames of the candles grow, reaching over a foot in height. Power fills the room as a wind picks up, bending the flames but not extinguishing them. "Now, let's try this a third time. I, Zadie Halovale, with the might of my ancestors behind me, call forth Charognis, guardian and gatekeeper of Hell. Stop fucking around and help me save Zevran."

She reaches for what appears to be a leash, floating before her, and yanks, seeing the three heads appearing before her, followed by the rest of his body, shrunk to fit into her dome of magic. "Now that's more like it."

Charognis growls and snaps at her only to feel his teeth bounce off a shield. "Now, that's not very nice of you." Zadie rises to her feet, meeting the hound at eye level. "You met me once, remember?"

"You summoned me. Deal with the consequences of an angry demon." His voice rumbles in anger as he lifts his lips to bare all three sets of teeth.

"I did. I doubt you would have answered if I had asked politely. A hound like you demands and respects strength. I showed it to you."

"What do you want?"

"I need an escort into Hell."

"No."

"I am not asking."

"Why?"

"To stop the engagement of Zevran."

"What makes you so sure you can stop it?" Charognis growls.

"I summoned you, didn't I? Zevran is MY mate, and Daddy Dearest is not taking that from me. Whether I am ready or not is beside the point. This has to be done."

Two sets of eyes study Zadie carefully, while one head diverts its gaze to Mordek, now standing in shock at what Zadie has done. "You let this happen?"

"I knew she was summoning, but not who until she said your name."

"She called three times. You had your chance to stop her."

Zadie claps her hands, drawing his attention back. "Standing right here! And Mordek was not getting in this bubble. Now, are you going to help me or not? All you need to do is get me there. I can take care of the rest."

They stare at each other, neither backing down, until Charognis huffs softly. "Fine. I'll take you there, but you are on your own in every way. I will not offer protection against other demons, nor King Draemorr."

Mordek stiffens at his words. "I will protect her. So will Zevran's Ashen-Guards."

"So be it. Let's go."

"Where are we meeting?"

"I will take her to the Gallows Tree. Get on."

Zadie smiles and moves to Charognis's side, pulling herself up onto his back like she's mounting a warhorse. Her fingers twine gently in his fur, carefully avoiding the snakes that writhe in his mane. "Thank you."

"Don't thank me yet. This very well could end in your death."

"It could," she says simply, "but it won't. Soot, take care of the place. I'll be back as soon as I can. Let's go, Char."

"I will, Zadie," Soot replies.

"Char." Charognis grumbles, though his ears flick back at the name. "Now you're even giving me nicknames." He fades from the mortal realm into Hell's territory, arriving beside what looks like an ancient oak tree. Instead of leaves, colored ribbons dangle from the branches, each one ending in a trinket.

Zadie slides off Charognis's back, her gaze locking on the tree. Power radiates from it, thick and oppressive. "What is this place? I can feel a dark aura around it."

Charognis doesn't answer and disappears as he said.

Mordek steps in beside her and answers her question. "The Gallows Tree. It's where damned souls hang like fruit, never rotting, never released. A prison for those too dangerous to be reborn or reshaped. The tree binds them in stasis, unable to fight, unable to flee."

Zadie's eyes travel upward, taking in the endless sweep of ribbons. "And each ribbon is a soul."

"Yes," Mordek says. "This tree is ancient. For thousands of years it has stood here, collecting the souls of those beyond even the damned."

"I see."

"Come. If you're going to do this, we need to get you to the castle." Mordek says.

Zadie nods, but her eyes linger on the ribbons. They shiver though there is no wind, and she wonders if the tree is watching her back. Dragging her attention off the tree, she turns it to the landscape below her, noticing they are on what appears to be a small mountain. Below her, she can see the market she visited before with

Zevran, the enormous dome she practiced in, or at least, she thinks it's the one, knowing there were several of them at different levels. Her eyes stray to the river winding around the castle before focusing on her destination. Realizing just how formidable the castle looks from this vantage point, with its slate-black stone and pointed crenellations, like claws or teeth reaching skyward. "It looks like a long walk."

"It's a good thing we are not walking. I can phase you right to the castle."

"Wait, you can? I thought you couldn't."

"I can't go through the gate between your realm and mine, but now that you are here, it's fair game." He offers his hand and waits as she takes it.

"I want to go to the gates. I need to walk in on my own and make an impression."

"Deal."

She reaches out to take his hand, a strange tingling flooding through her body momentarily, before finding herself staring at the iron gates she last saw with Zevran. Glancing past the gate, she recognizes a few faces from the last time she was here, recalling what Zevran said. None of them can be trusted. Taking a breath, she glances at Mordek. "You can fade."

"Are you sure?"

"Yes, it's best if you are not seen with me."

"I will be nearby." His body breaks into pieces, hovering for a moment, before disappearing from her sight, all but a pair of red eyes.

Chapter Twenty-Two

The Reckoning

Taking a deep breath, she squares her shoulders and walks through the gates, spotting the two guards stepping forward. Smiling sweetly, she offers a slight bow. "I am here for the party. I believe it said, *The father extends an invitation to all,* and I am part of *the all.*"

"You are a mortal."

"That's right."

"How did you get here?"

"A taxi."

Their eyes narrow as their grip on their pole-arms tightens, straightening their bodies to full height, hoping to intimidate this mortal that dares to mock them. "A taxi, you say?"

Zadie's eyes flash, her fingertips sparking with lightning as she faces them squarely. "Unless you want to end up as popsicles like your friends did, I wouldn't suggest it, boys. Are they still encased in ice, or have you figured out how to thaw them?"

"That was you?"

"Indeed. Now, are you going to let me pass?"

They both step back, gesturing to the party. "Enjoy."

"I intend to." Zadie meanders through the front gardens, letting her senses sweep over the crowd, cataloguing the desires of everyone. Who intends to stand in her way? Who doesn't care that she's even here? She meets the gazes turned her way, reading them like open books; confusion, recognition, hostility. An entire spectrum of emotions, and none of which surprise her.

She pauses before a cluster of screaming nightshades. They snap and hiss at her fingers, sharp leaves rattling like teeth. Chuckles rise around her as if they're waiting for the plants to bite the mortal. Instead, she releases her magic and wraps it around the wild greenery. The nightshades still beneath her touch, a soft hum spills from their throats. Gasps echo behind her, but Zadie only snickers. Leaning close, she whispers so only they can hear. "Good little Beastlies. Behave now. No screaming for Zadie. Daddy needs to hear me."

The plants quiver, obedient, and she turns toward the looming double doors. Last time they were open, but today, they are closed now. Why? Did Zevran's father know she was coming? Her eyes flick to the guards at the side entrance, checking everyone entering. Damn prophets probably warned him. Was she the shadow Soot spoke of? If not, she intends to be. No one is marrying Zevran but her.

Ignoring the whispers questioning who she is, and how she tamed the nightshades, Zadie reaches the ironwood doors. Her fingers trace the carvings, lingering on Zevran's likeness before drifting toward his father's etched face. That arrogant expression stirs her anger like a spark to tinder. "Daddy Dearest. We need to talk."

She taps his wooden nose once. Twice. Thrice. Power flares, flooding from her hand into the carving, and the doors burst apart in a storm of splintered wood. Shards whirl around her in a glittering cloud; the thunder of her entrance is unmistakable.

When it settles, Zadie stands there, dressed to kill, hands on her hips and eyes narrowed dangerously on the King. "King Draemorr." Her voice drips with sarcasm. "I heard there was a party, and it seems my invite was misplaced or misdirected. You wouldn't have anything to do with that, would you?"

She spares a glance at Zevran, sitting in a chair next to him, bound by invisible magical chains. Next to him is a stunning female, dressed in the skankiest gown Zadie has ever seen, her hands roaming possessively up Zevran's thighs.

Zadie grits her teeth and clenches her fists, not willing to do anything drastic yet. Her voice shifts, filled with challenge. "Get your hands off my Mate, Veyra.

Zevran belongs to me, and no blonde bimbo succubus is taking him from me."

"Zadie!" Zevran calls out.

Draemorr lifts his hand. "Silence!" His voice booms across the room. "No mortal is allowed in my court."

"If you take the invisible chains off him and give him back, I will happily leave." She acknowledges the surrounding murmur, seeing some of the demons that had scattered at the door exploding, now looking Zevran's way.

"Mortals," Draemorr scoffs. "And their crazy ideas."

"It's not crazy if it's true. Take them off or I will."

"You think a human..." His voice drips with distaste. "...is going to stop me?"

"Think? I *think* you have it wrong. I AM going to stop you."

"Guards! Seize her."

Zadie quickly scans the room, seeing a swarm of guards coming her way. Knowing she has limited time, she cups her hand and blows on it. Glitter billows out towards the thrones, latching onto the magical bindings, identifying them for the others to see. Knowing her magic will eat through the bindings, she turns to the first guards approaching, just as Mordek appears beside her.

"Ashen-Guards. Protect the mate-bonded Princess." Mordek calls out, seeing them phase in throughout the room.

"Who says I need protection?" Zadie mutters and calls forth three tiny balls of fire. Ignoring the laughter surrounding her, she sends them out at the closest guards, watching as they expand and engulf them, dropping the guards to the ground as they roll around in agony, the fire burning through their skin.

The laughter around her silences, each demon now scattering away from the mortal in the middle of the room, not wanting to earn the wrath of someone who could actually hurt them.

Zadie stalks forward towards the throne, watching Veyra shift nervously and her eyes dart up to the king. Clearly, it's a silent plea asking for help. "I am not telling you again, Veyra. GET away from him and you might live." Seeing movement at her right, she waves her hand in an arc, a wall of flame spreading from her fingertips. The guards scream and stagger back, unwilling to get any closer.

On her left side, she calls forth a blue rune. Swirling her finger through it, she splits it into three and sends the small sigils outwards. Each one strikes a guard, who stares at what is now affixed to their chest. Ice fractures and spreads outwards rapidly, encasing them within seconds.

She returns her attention to the throne, laughter spilling from her lips at the King's expression; his jaw ticking, the wide eyes, the extra redness of frustration across his cheeks. More like a cornered or panicked animal than the King of Hell. "What's the matter, Draemorr? Scared of a little mortal? You should be. You are giving away what is rightfully mine. Now, be a good king and return him. Actually…" She trails off, her gaze shifting to the bindings, stalling for another few seconds. "He can return himself."

Feeling his binds break, Zevran grabs Veyra's hand, snapping her fingers as he removes them from his thigh. "Not yours. I don't know what magic you used to enthrall my father, but it was NEVER going to work on me, because I have found my mate and she's standing out there, fighting for me." He rises and jumps off the raised dais. "Zadie, my love."

Draemorr growls at his son's movements. "Zevran, get back here now. You will marry Veyra as I commanded."

"No, Father. Since you made this a public spectacle, so will I. Zadie is my mate. She proved that when she broke your bindings. Only a true mate can overpower the King's command. I will ONLY accept her. If you won't, then consider me disowned." He continues forward and engulfs Zadie in a hug, locking his arms around her. "Zadie, my love. You came for me."

"Of course I came for you. You are mine. No succu'bitch is touching you again."

He lifts a hand, wrapping it around the back of her neck, his thumb caressing just below her earlobe. He lowers his head, his lips crashing against hers, claiming her, before she can pull away.

The moment they touch, Zadie staggers under both the emotions washing over her at his lips on her and the power of her curse breaking, flooding from her in waves of raw energy.

Pressure rolls through the chamber, crushing the air from every lung, rattling bones and steel. The flames in the braziers flare white-gold, and holy brilliance floods the room. For a moment, the black stone gleams like marble. Flawless.

Before the shockwave knocks them over, scattering the ash and bone.

Demon's roar against it, reveling in the raw force encompassing the room.

The nightshades outside shriek like a thousand banshees, their roots tearing free and their vines convulsing upward as blossoms burst open in a flood of blackened blood-red petals. Thunder rolls across the skies, rattling through the walls of the castle as if Heaven itself has hurled down judgment. The castle's windows shatter, shards spraying outward in a storm of razors, causing demons to snarl and stagger back, shielding their faces, as the pieces sliced their skin.

Zevran's grip only tightens as the world breaks around them, lost to the feel of his mate in his arms. Something he has been craving since the day he met her in the coffee shop. Even before that, if he thought about it, but that thought is far from his mind as emotions have taken over.

Then comes the silence.

For one, impossible heartbeat, Hell itself stills. Every sound swallowed into a void. Magic dissipates. Even the nightshades grow silent with nary a scream. And then the world exhales in a detonating boom, the force of it splintering the floor beneath their feet in a web of cracks. Shadows claw up the walls, writhing and convulsing like living things before slamming back into place. Turrets plunge to the ground, stone skittering across the ground on impact.

And through it all, Zadie glows. A ripple of celestial light spills across her skin, a shimmer that brands itself in every demon's memory before fading. Not mortal. Not entirely human.

When the glow ebbs, she breaks from the kiss, her chest heaving as she lifts her gaze to the copper ones she has grown to love. She whispers softly, claiming Zevran, the same way he claimed her with the kiss. "Mine."

Around them, the castle trembles, demons cower and whisper in awe, fear, and hunger. Even the king feels the veil lifted from his eyes.

Zevran presses his forehead to hers, voice raw, reverent. "Yours."

Zadie smiles, her eyes sliding past him to his father, standing on the throne, stunned at the damage to his castle. "Do you think Daddy Dearest gets it now?"

"He might, but that doesn't matter right now. You've undone it, Zadie. No more curses. Just you and me, together, forever."

"Wait, do you feel that?"

"I just feel you, Zadie."

"No, it's something else." She tilts her head, sensing.

Not rage. Not wrath. Attention.

It feels like the stillness before dawn, a quiet weight pressing down on the room. A pulse of awareness that brushes over Zadie's skin, lingering like fingers tracing the threads of her soul. The presence does not strike, does not scorn; it only watches. Curious. Patient. Waiting. The kiss has not only freed Zadie and Zevran; it has called something older awake, and it has turned its gaze upon them. When the weight lifts, she is left with the unsettling certainty: a god knows her name now.

"Hmmm, something for another day."

"Yes, it is."

"Since there is a wedding planned, Zadie, my love. Will you marry me?"

"I will."

"Great!" He clasps her hand and turns them both to face his father. "Father. Zadie said yes!"

As the magic lifts from him, Draemorr's shoulders slump, suddenly realizing that if he wants to keep his son as heir apparent, then it means that Zadie and him are a package deal. He steps down from the dais and approaches them, taking mental note of the chaos surrounding him and the repairs he is going to need to do.

Stopping a few feet away, he meets his son's gaze, reading the happiness within, before shifting over to hers, where a mix of defiance and daring faced him. "Zadie, I am sorry for doubting you. If you are who Zevran chooses, I will accept it. All I ask is that you do not crash my parties and destroy my castle again."

Zadie smiles cooly, stiffening at his acceptance. "Leave me off the guest list again, and I cannot guarantee it."

Draemorr chuckles. "You definitely have spirit, as well as power. I can see why you were paired with my son. Welcome to the family, Zadie."

"Before I accept, I want confirmation you will not be sending my ex after me again. Also, you owe me a new fucking dock and car! An expensive one since mine is a melted metal art piece now."

Zevran snaps his gaze between them. "What?"

"Apparently," Zadie narrows her eyes again at Draemorr. "He sent my ex to kill me. The one that self-combusted. He melted my car and destroyed my dock."

"To be fair, *you* blew up your dock when you obliterated him. Nice play there, by the way. I apologize. I was wrong and not perceiving things clearly. My wedding gift to you is a new car and dock."

Zevran growls, his arm tightening around her waist. "No, you were under a spell that Veyra enthralled you with."

"I see that now; she will be dealt with."

"Good." Zevran turns back to Zadie, running a finger along her cheek. "I was not kidding when I said we can make it today, Zadie. A wedding was planned." He slides a look his father's way, "without my consent, but we can make use of it."

"Son... you know I only had your best interests. It was about time you settled down."

Zevran mutters. "Yes, with someone of your choosing, not mine."

"As you said, magic was involved. When this first started, I had not intended to force you. I apologize."

"There's the father I know... Speaking of which, where is that snake, Veyra?"

Zadie smiles, squeezing his hand gently. "She scurried out of the hall with her tail between her legs when she realized she lost."

"She won't give up easily."

Zadie shrugs her shoulders. "Then I will kill her, over and over, until she realizes who is going to win."

"Oh, so NOW you believe you can't kill me," Zevran teases her.

"Yes, well, we mortals have limitations."

Draemorr gives another glance around his hall. "More than mortal. I can feel the taint of celestialness."

"Taint?" Zadie arches a brow.

Chuckling, he raises his hand in defence. "Yes, taint. You know we are always at war with the celestial court, just as they are with us."

"True. Perhaps our binding will change that. Especially since I have celestial ancestry."

"Only time will tell. Now. Before any more of my guests disperse, we should get you married. Unless of course you can fix this mess first?"

"Unfortunately no. I can thaw your guards out though."

"That's fine. I will bring in mages to repair it." He turns back to Zevran. "I will say it's unexpected, but let's get the Oath Weaver in here to bind you."

Zevran chuckles, watching his father walk away. He spins Zadie to face him, staring into her eyes. "My match made in heaven."

Zadie laughs, nudging his shoulder. "As I said when we first met, more like a romantic Hellstorm."

"And As I answered, that's the nicest thing anyone's ever said to me." He replies, his arms wrapping around her as his lips find hers once more.

Chapter Twenty-Three

Epilogue

Elsewhere, in a small cottage, a black cat purrs on a windowsill, basking in the sunshine as a portal opens behind him and a shrouded figure peers through. "Soot."

Soot lifts his head, his amber gaze shifting over to the woman. "Headmistress Morgrim."

"Is it done?"

"Yes, Princess Zadie of the Celestial Court and Prince Zevren of the Demonic Court have had their souls reunited and have been mate-matched. A match made between worlds that will usher in a new era for humanity."

"Well done, Soot."

"Don't thank me. Thank Supernatural Soulmates. They are the ones that paired them."

"I am..."

"That better not get out, Headmistress. I have a reputation to uphold." Soot drops his head, a cheshire grin spreading across his features as he curls up once more.

"It won't." The portal closes, leaving the cottage in silence once more.

Soot lifts his gaze, his eyes glowing softly as words scrawl upon the computer before lowering his head once more to catnap.

The Kiss That Cracked Hell

Forget Veyra. Forget royal duty. Zevran, chained by oath and spell, rescued not by guards, nor by blood, but by the mortal witch the King tried to leash. Tonight, she walked straight into the Iron Court, shattered the ballroom, and everyone's expectations. Fire, ice, and fury. She freed the Hellion Prince with her own hands. And when their lips finally met in choice and defiance, Hell itself broke. If love makes rulers... has Hell just crowned its future?

The end

For the cursed, the reckless, and the ones who won't stay on their leash.
May your Hellhounds burn and your wards hold strong.

Chapter Twenty-Five

People

Zadie - White blonde hair Cobalt eyes (28)
Soot - Familiar - Black cat
Josh - Ex Boyfriend
Elliot - Ex Boyfriend
Desmond Rasgar - Ex Boyfriend
Nim - Friend
Draemorr - King of Hell
Zevran - Prince of Hell
Talaris - Rogue of Hell
Drewgare - Fighter brother
Kharan - Brother
Rurik - Youngest Brother
Eryndria - Oldest Sister
Lucilla - Youngest Sister
Mordek, Thane, Nicx, Pyrrh, Skarix - Ashen-Guard
Ramone - Chef
Charognis - Guardian between
Veyra Baelgrith - Succubus
Malacia - Sister
House Algonod - Dukes of Desire
Trezzek's - War Dogs

Lady Seraphine Netherax

Lord Veyric Cindral

House Tagrech

The Triune of Spite

Lord Xorgol of the Eastern Hemisphere

Auntie Athena

Monica - Child in Wraithmore

Chapter Twenty-Six

Contributors

.

Cover Design - Infixgraph Designs
Beta readers - M Verronneau, T Parkin
Arc reader - A Wathley, L Van Hout
Editor - N Peterman, M Harris, J Pettigrew
Editing Software - ProWritingAid, Google Docs, Impact, Atticus
Assists - C Moore, M Harris, T Parkin, H Roberts, M Beers
Author Portrait - G Woodward

About the Author

Randi lives in Victoria, BC. Canada. She is a dog groomer by day and a writer/gamer/reader by night. She partook in the SCA and taught medieval dance for fifteen years. From 2004 until 2022, she attended the Faerie festival annually, keeping fantasy alive in her heart. With multiple books published, she hopes they will draw you away from the modern world and into a land of intrigue and fantasy, where magic, dragons, shifters, fae, vampires and kings roam the lands.

Additional Information

T hank you for taking the time to read my stories and I hope that you enjoyed them. If you have, below is a list of my other books. Please feel free to follow me, or add me via Goodreads or Facebook. Also, reviews are important to self published authors, so please take the time to leave one. Thank you.

Social Media

www.facebook.com/AuthorRandiAnneDey
www.facebook.com/groups/randiswriting
www.goodreads.com/author/show/45347028.Randi_Anne_Dey
www.amazon.com/author/randiannedey

Published books

The King's Mystic: Oct 2023
The Dragon's Mystic: May 2024
Cantara's Mystic: Apr 2025
Madison's Web: Mar 2024
Dragonscales Divide: Nov 2024
Chahaya Durmada: Five Swords of Power: Eta 2025
Fae Guardians Poppy: May 2025
You Stole my Shroom: July 2025
Dance, Little Dove: Nov 2025
Dating the Damned: Oct 2025
Royal Deception: Tails Scales and Tiaras Anthology June 2024
The Emperor's Violet: Cabs and Crime Anthology Sept 2025

www.ingramcontent.com/pod-product-compliance
Lightning Source LLC
Chambersburg PA
CBHW070956120726
47910CB00004B/1258